Christmas Rapping...

When a rap group clashes with three traditional carolers, the results are truly inspiring.

The Bracelet...

Very pricey diamond jewelry is only for the rich, but a young lady of modest means may discover a different kind of treasure.

The Crystal Silver China Club...

When five temporary employees throw a very special holiday party, they discover their job has a hidden benefit.

The Twelve Shopping Days of Christmas...

Can a personalized shopper accommodate the wacky wishes of a wealthy client...when his requests include a partridge in a pear tree?

The Christmas Store

Ray Sipherd

ST. MARTIN'S PAPERBACKS

THE CHRISTMAS STORE

Copyright © 1993 by Ray Sipherd.

All rights reserved. No part of this book may be used or reproduced in any manner whatsoever without written permission except in the case of brief quotations embodied in critical articles or reviews. For information address St. Martin's Press, 175 Fifth Avenue, New York, N.Y. 10010.

Library of Congress Catalog Card Number: 93-24294

ISBN: 0-312-95308-9

Printed in the United States of America

St. Martin's Press hardcover edition/October 1993
St. Martin's Paperbacks edition/November 1994

10 9 8 7 6 5 4 3 2 1

For Mother and Dad

CONTENTS

TALES OF THE
CHRISTMAS STORE

*W*elcome to the Christmas Store!" . . .
"Yes, madam. You'll find Ladies' Dresses straight
ahead." . . . "Winter coats for gentlemen—third aisle on
your left." . . . "So many packages! Here, let me hold the
door." . . . "And the happiest of holidays to all of
you!" . . .

How often have I said these words and others like
them to the crowds who fill this great department store?

My name is Thomas Cavanaugh. Customers and
clerks alike consider me a customer relations representative—or what in former years was known as a floor-
walker. As for my physical appearance, I am of average
height and weight. With my black hair and clear blue
eyes, I am considered moderately handsome. My attire is
usually a dark blue pin-striped suit. Three points of a
white silk handkerchief are visible in my breast pocket.

My shirts are from an English shirtmaker; my ties are mostly French. I have been told, in fact, that I am the very model of the well-dressed gentleman.

For years I was employed in the Gentlemen's Apparel section of the store. Then five years ago I assumed a new position as a sort of walking guide and customer assistance person. From the day after Thanksgiving to the night of Christmas Eve, I move continually among the aisles, endeavoring to make the holidays as pleasant as I can for all I meet. Does a shopper seek directions to a particular department? I'm the man to ask. For no one knows this store as well as I.

And what a spectacle of color and activity is to be found within the store at Christmastime! Here, everywhere I look are tables, shelves, and counters piled high with merchandise of every kind. Here, galaxies of small lights twinkle from the ceilings. Here, scents of powders, perfumes, and colognes take on the properties of magical elixirs. Here, the babble of a thousand voices is counterpointed by the melodies of carols carried on the air. It is for reasons such as these that I delight in calling this the Christmas Store.

Yet as night approaches and the closing hour of the store draws near, I watch the customers collect their purchases and head in the direction of the exit doors. I watch as salespeople tote up their final figures for the day, retrieve their coats, and hurry also for the doors toward home. How fortunate they are to have someone awaiting them at home when they arrive. I envy them. For I have no one; no wife to greet me, no family to surround me at the conclusion of a long and weary day.

Instead, soon after the last clerks have departed for the night, I make my way to the Stationery section of the store. There, at the far end of a hallway off the sales floor, I approach an old and rather battered metal cabinet. Inside it are some rolls of cash register tape of the sort found on those hand-cranked models no longer in use. Other shelves are occupied by boxes full of carbon paper, stacks of typing paper yellowing around the edges, plus a quantity of 2B pencils, all without a sharpened point.

Pressed against the inner right-hand corner of a lower shelf, however, is a leatherbound portfolio. It, too, shows the neglect of time. The brown moroccan leather face is dull and brittle to the touch. Within the portfolio, when it is opened, is a large, lined writing pad.

Each night, I withdraw the portfolio and return to the now-deserted sales floor. There, along one wall, is a small French writing desk. The desk itself is covered with a variety of objects—Lucite paperweights, pearl-handled letter openers, onyx pen and pencil holders, and the like. Having moved them to one side, I draw up a fruitwood desk chair and sit down. I open the portfolio and take from my suit pocket a fountain pen, which I keep filled with indelible black ink. I place the nib of it down on the pad. Then I begin to write.

At nine P.M., the uniformed security guards of the evening shift begin arriving on the floor. When they first found me sitting here, they regarded me with curiosity, but did not speak. Likely, they assumed I was a member of the sales staff who had remained to finish necessary paperwork. But after those initial nights of simply glancing at me with uncertainty, they became accustomed to my presence as they went on about their rounds. Always, I return their greetings affably.

Soon after the departure of the guards, the men and

women of the cleaning staff appear. At once, they set to vacuuming the floor and dusting and tidying the shelves and countertops. They also probably assume I am a salesclerk, even the section manager, forced by the increased holiday activity to stay on and record the business of the day.

In one sense they are right. But what I have been putting down on paper every night since I began is not a tally of the day's receipts. I keep a record, yes—but of the people and events that I have witnessed in my wanderings about the store. On these pages also, I have included vignettes told to me by others whose reliability I trust. Some of these accounts are fanciful, others strain credulity. Still, I write them all.

So it is that in the quiet hours of the evening, as the holidays draw near, I return to the Stationery section, fetch the leatherbound portfolio, and write as faithfully and entertainingly as possible what I have seen or heard. As I reread the stories, many bring a smile of remembered pleasure; some, a sadness that is made more poignant by the universal joy of the holidays against which they occur. But in one manner or another, each has found a fond place in my heart.

Here, then, are my tales of the Christmas Store.

THE
BRACELET

*F*orget fingers, forget earlobes, forget necks. Wrists were Nicholas's specialty. Let other salesclerks extol the qualities of rings, earrings, and necklaces: Nicholas knew bracelets best of anyone in the Fine Jewelry department of the store. So it was that when a woman appeared opposite him at his counter, the young man looked directly at her wrists before examining the rest of her. That done, he would slowly lift his eyes to hers and gaze with feeling several silent moments before telling her which bracelet on display would complement her beauty best. Even those women who were somewhat less than beautiful by common standards were made to feel so when touched by his words. Nicholas, it hardly need be added, was a most successful salesman.

A personable fellow in his mid-twenties, he had been employed by the store for several years. It was no disadvantage either to his mercantile talents that, with his thick black hair, deep-set hazel eyes, and aquiline features, his attentions were sought after by the female customers who frequented Fine Jewelry.

But Nicholas also had a genuine affinity and fondness for his work. Each day as he took his place behind the display cases filled with trays and open jeweler's boxes, he looked forward to holding in his hands bracelets of incalculable worth. Here, adorning silver, gold, and platinum bands, were diamonds, sapphires, and rubies: emeralds from Zambia; pearls from Tahiti; aquamarines and amethysts; coral and kunzite; turquoise and tourmalines and tsavorites and topaz. Nicholas was fond of boasting to his fellow clerks that for every woman's wrist there was the perfect bracelet waiting to be clasped around it, and his record of finding one to match the other was exceptionally good. Until today.

It was the morning of the first day of December and he found himself confronted by the very thin and very delicate wrists of a young woman. The hands and fingers were delicate as well, with tiny blue veins showing through the skin. Adjusting his attention slightly, he saw that the cuffs that fell just above the wrists belonged to a simple brown cloth coat. The young woman was possibly a file clerk or a domestic. He knew that once he told her what the prices of the bracelets were, she'd murmur an apology and go away.

Still, with a practiced smile, he raised his head—and discovered he was looking at one of the most innocent faces he had ever seen. She was not beautiful in the sense that some of the wealthy and elegantly dressed women shoppers were. She wore no makeup. Her hair was brown and cut straight above the collar of her coat. But it was her eyes that Nicholas particularly noticed. They were the color of pure amber. Nicholas had never looked at—or been looked at by—eyes such as those that faced him now.

"I'd like to see a bracelet," the young woman said.

"Certainly," Nicholas answered. He smiled again. "Perhaps something in sterling silver."

"No. That one," the young woman said. She placed her index finger on the countertop and pointed downward through the glass.

Nicholas looked down at the shelf just below the countertop. Arrayed across it was a variety of jeweled bracelets, each one set with many precious stones. But at the very center of them, lying in a silk-lined jeweler's box, was a bracelet that was the most magnificent of all. The design was of twelve angels with their wings outspread. Their gowns and bodies were of 18 karat gold, as were their halos. Still, it was the angels' wings themselves that made the piece particularly glorious. Each pair contained what looked like hundreds of small diamonds that shimmered dazzlingly in the light.

To Nicholas the bracelet was a supreme example of the jeweler's art. He also knew it was by far the most expensive bracelet the department had to sell. Since it was first displayed a month ago many people had exclaimed over its beauty and design, and some had even asked the price. Once told, they generally expelled a little gasp, repeated what a truly splendid piece of jewelry it was, and moved on with some haste toward other sections of the store.

Finally Nicholas looked up. "That one?" he asked.

"Yes. Please." She said no more.

"Um. Yes, of course."

With a sigh, Nicholas turned and stepped to a cabinet beneath the register, and pulled open a drawer. From it he withdrew a key, and returned to the display case. He unlocked the sliding panel on his side of the case and moved the panel to one side. He reached in with a hand, grasped the open box in which the bracelet lay, lifted it, and placed it on the countertop nearer to himself than her. He also held the box with both hands, ready to protect the bracelet in the event she tried to snatch it suddenly. She didn't look the sort to attempt anything so foolish, he thought, but at this season thieves were everywhere.

To his relief, the young woman made no gesture toward the bracelet. When she did, it was to incline her head and stare down at it in silent awe.

Nicholas said nothing. But as she continued to examine it, he examined her. It confirmed what he'd believed at first. In no way could she afford expensive jewelry, least of all this bracelet that had mesmerized her so.

Then, slowly, her right arm slid across the countertop toward Nicholas. With her other hand she pulled up the sleeve of her coat until the wrist was fully visible.

"I would like to try it on." She raised her head and smiled. "Please."

Nicholas was certain now it was a scam. Once the bracelet had been clasped around her wrist she'd flee. He wondered if an accomplice waited for her on the street outside. To his relief, he saw a security guard standing fewer than fifteen feet away.

"May I?" Now her arm was lifted, pointed toward him.

"Yes, of course," he said. He took the bracelet by

the ends, drew it up, then clasped and locked it firmly, circling her outstretched wrist.

Once more she bowed her head and stared at the bracelet. Her eyes began to mist. "It's beautiful," she whispered.

"Quite," Nicholas agreed.

"Does it have a name?"

"A name?" The question puzzled Nicholas. "Not that I know of."

She rotated her wrist, first to one side, then the other, studying the tiny figures. "Then I'll call it my angel bracelet. And I'll give each one of them a name. I'll start with Gabriel, and Michael, Raphael, and Uriel. They were the four archangels. Did you know that?"

Nicholas shook his head.

"I like Michael best. Is your name Michael?"

"Nicholas."

She shrugged, then raised her arm above her head to let the facets of the diamonds of the bracelet sparkle in the lights.

As Nicholas watched her, several explanations of the young woman's strange behavior became clear. The first was that she had misread the price tag on the bracelet, and mistakenly believed she was in the section that sold costume jewelry. Another was that she was a young eccentric heiress who affected an ingenious demeanor and dressed in secondhand clothes so as to circulate about the store anonymously while she shopped.

Lowering her arm, the young woman now moved down the counter to a large lighted magnifying glass attached to a stand. She placed the bracelet under it, and again turned her wrist this way and that while peering down into the glass.

"Excuse me," Nicholas said, after some moments. "Am I to assume you are considering the purchase of the bracelet?"

"Possibly," she answered, without looking up. More turning of the wrist.

"Well, then, may I suggest—"

"Yes. It's very possible," she interrupted him. "But not today."

"Still, if you're at all interested in the piece, perhaps you'd like to leave your name."

She looked up at him and smiled. "No, I'd rather not. You understand."

"Of course," he said. In fact, he was more baffled than before.

The young woman placed her right arm on the counter facing him. "If you would be so kind as to undo the clasp."

He nodded, and did as she had asked. Taking the bracelet, he laid it in the silk-lined box and restored it to the shelf. Only when he had locked the case did Nicholas look up.

She was gone.

By mid-morning of the next day she was gone from Nicholas's mind as well. The sheer volume of shoppers, browsers, and the curious he had to serve consumed every moment of his time. Among those he sought to help was an anorexic lady with a pointed nose and coal-black eyes whose face uncannily resembled the fox on the fur collar of the coat she wore. There was also a prince from somewhere unpronounceable, a short and heavily wrapped man, who seemed about to purchase every bracelet on display until he was dissuaded by a member of his entourage. In fact, throughout the day, Nicholas tried more bracelets on more wrists than on any day he could recall.

It startled him, therefore, to look up from the counter shortly before closing time that night and see her standing in precisely the same spot where she had stood the day before.

"Hi." She smiled. "Do you remember me?"

He nodded. "Yes, I do." His voice remained pleasant but impassive. He quickly checked his watch. "We're closing in five minutes."

"Yes, I know. I couldn't come before now. May I see it?"

He knew he didn't have to ask her what she meant by "it."

"I won't be long. I promise," she assured him. "Please?"

Nodding, Nicholas retrieved the key to the display case, unlocked it, slid back the panel, and brought up the box in which the angel bracelet lay. As he placed it on the countertop, she extended her right arm toward him, palm upward, wrist exposed.

As he had done the day before, he lifted the two ends of the bracelet from the box, drew them up around her wrist, and clasped them.

And as she had done the day before, she raised her arm to let the facets of the diamonds catch the light. "It's beautiful."

"Yes. Very," he said.

Once more, she placed the bracelet underneath the lighted magnifier, studying the angels one by one.

Behind her, waves of shoppers headed toward the exit doors; she took no notice. Finally, she turned to Nicholas and held out her arm again in his direction. He removed the bracelet and restored it to the box.

"Thank you," the young woman said, and quickly disappeared into the departing crowd.

As he closed the box and locked it in the case, he wondered if she would return.

He decided that she would.

He was right.

The next morning, soon after the store opened, she was there facing him across the countertop. She also came the next day—and the next.

And each day the routine was the same. If Nicholas was engaged with other customers, the young woman would wait patiently until the moment he was free. Then with her fingers she would lightly touch his arm. "Excuse me. May I—?" followed by Nicholas's nod. The key, the case unlocked, the box displayed, the bracelet clasped about the wrist, the upraised arm, the scrutiny beneath the magnifying glass . . . "It's beautiful." Day after day.

By the beginning of the second week, Nicholas admitted to himself that he was irked. As more people filled the store and activity increased, he resented having to take precious time in which he could be making real sales to indulge one particular young woman for whom the bracelet had become a fantasy that bordered on obsession. He had already decided she was not a thief. But he had also given up the notion that she was an heiress in disguise. He'd wondered briefly if she was a person hired by the store, and who was posing as a customer to test the salespeople on their helpfulness and patience. He soon decided she was simply too naïve for such a job.

It wasn't that she lacked intelligence. Beneath her naïveté he sensed a sharp, even calculating mind. And each day as he clasped the bracelet to her wrist and witnessed her expression of delight, he, too, began to share her happiness. In fact, as Nicholas lay awake one night, he acknowledged that for all her guilelessness, there was a pure and simple joy to her that few people possessed. That night also, he admitted to himself—with an honesty that both surprised and troubled him—that he looked forward to her visit the next day.

Yet by noon the young woman was nowhere to be seen. Closing time arrived and she had not appeared. Nor did she appear on the next day, nor the day after that. By the fourth day, Nicholas decided to skip his lunch break, to be on duty, if she chose that time to come. But she did not.

So it was with a feeling of intense relief the morning following, just as a wall of shoppers at his counter parted, that he saw her standing in the aisle facing him.

"You're here—!" he started, and wasn't sure what else to say.

"I'm sorry. I was sick. The flu. I couldn't come."

"I . . . I hope you're feeling better now," he said at last.

"Yes. Thank you."

"The bracelet?" he asked.

"Please, if I may."

The key obtained, the case unlocked, the panel slid aside, the box that bore the angel bracelet placed upon the countertop . . .

That night it rained. By dawn the weather had turned colder, covering the streets and sidewalks with a glaze of ice. Still, Nicholas arrived earlier than usual, and long before the other clerks appeared.

After hanging up his coat and scarf, he went directly to the storage cabinet where the boxes used to display jewelry were kept. Searching among them, he found one with a plush interior of deep blue quilted velvet that he believed would show off the beauty of the angel bracelet all the more.

Then from its place in the display case, he removed the bracelet. Placing it gently on a chamois cloth, he cleaned it with a special jeweler's solvent, carefully drying it with cotton swabs so that no moisture remained. With another cloth he polished the gold of the bracelet to a glowing sheen. That done, he gently laid it on its velvet bed within the box.

Looking at the bracelet one last time before restoring it to the display case, Nicholas was amused by the irony of what he had just done. By cleaning and polishing the bracelet as he had, it appeared of even greater worth than the enormous price already placed on it. And he had done it for a young woman whose name he didn't know, and who in no way could afford to purchase it.

But neither of those things mattered to him in the least. What mattered only was the happiness her daily visits brought him.

And as the days drew ever nearer Christmas Day itself, it mattered to him more and more.

It was December 21, the winter solstice. Yet contrary to the calendar, the weather turned unseasonably mild, bringing even more customers into the store.

Nicholas arrived in a buoyant mood, still humming a Christmas carol he had heard a street musician playing on his way to work.

He was about to assume his position behind the counter when an idea came to him. Taking a small white tag from a box that sat next to the register, he wrote the word HOLD on it in large letters. Beneath that he scribbled a fictitious name. A little string accompanied the tag, and Nicholas tied it firmly to the bracelet. He knew that another clerk, on discovering the tag, would believe a customer was seriously interested in buying it, and therefore would not show the bracelet to any other customer. When the young woman appeared later in the day, Nicholas would hastily explain that since he had written out the tag himself, the bracelet would remain for as long a time as she desired to come here and admire it.

Nicholas now took the key to the display case. He walked briskly to the case, still humming the carol, unlocked the case, and slid the panel back. He reached into the top shelf and stretched his hand to take the box. What his fingers touched instead was cold hard glass. He moved his hand to one side, then the other. After a minute of finding nothing he withdrew his hand, stood up, and leaned over the countertop. He closed his eyes, praying silently that when he opened them the fear that had already seized him would be put to rest.

It wasn't.

When he looked down through the glass at last, he saw that the angel bracelet and the box in which it lay were gone.

It had to be somewhere, he assured himself. Grabbing still more keys, he went from one case to the next throughout the section, peering, reading, hoping—finding nothing of the bracelet anywhere he searched.

By now, the other clerks who had arrived were setting out the stock, preparing for the day's activities. Nicholas moved among them quickly, inquiring whether any customer had asked to see the angel bracelet yesterday. A few clerks remembered just such inquiries at a time when he was on a break, and one said he had exhibited the bracelet for a diamond-bedecked dowager. Another clerk admitted he had pointed out the splendid features of the angel bracelet to a wealthy older gentleman, who at her urging had allowed his young female companion to try it on her wrist. A third remembered that the manager of Fine Jewelry himself—who unexpectedly was taking a vacation day today—had been seen quietly studying the bracelet shortly before closing time last night.

"Hello."

Nicholas heard her voice behind him as he was talking to yet another clerk. The moment he had feared had come. He took a deep breath, trying to mask the awful emptiness he felt, and turned around.

"Hello," he said. At once, his mouth went dry as ashes, and he became conscious of a slight tremor in his hand.

"It isn't there," the girl said. Her face showed no concern, but merely puzzlement, as if she, too, assumed the bracelet had been temporarily moved from its accustomed place.

"I know," he said. "It's gone."

"Gone?"

His mind raced. What was there to tell her? "Yesterday—last night—I found some stones were loose. We sent it to an outside jeweler to be fixed."

"When will it be back?"

"Perhaps—well, it all depends—"

"Tomorrow?"

"Oh, no. Not tomorrow. With the holidays so close . . ."

Nicholas saw doubt, then fear, begin to fill her eyes. He rushed on with his lie. "But, maybe—I could have it back tomorrow. Late."

She pursed her lips and looked at him for several moments, as if trying to decide whether what he said was true. At last, she smiled with relief.

"I'm so glad," she said. "When you told me it was gone, I was afraid—"

She stopped, then put her fingers lightly on his hand. "I'll come tomorrow then."

Before Nicholas could answer, she had disappeared into the crowd.

The next day was the busiest the store had known. Hour upon hour, without respite, Nicholas and his fellow clerks attended to the customers who swept in with the intensity of waves at flood tide, splashed down their money, and receded with whatever gems and jeweled pieces lay in reach. How unlike them the young woman was, he thought. Certainly she knew that she would never in her life possess the angel bracelet as her own. She came simply to experience the bracelet's beauty for its own sake, and to find pleasure in the adoration of it, as one stands in reverence and awe before a masterpiece of art.

Now the bracelet was gone; sold probably, with no recollection by the other clerks of who the buyer was. But even so, if Nicholas should somehow learn the purchaser's identity, then what? Could he go to him or her, explain the girl's fascination for the bracelet, and attempt to buy it back? Impossible.

By midday, Nicholas had finally faced the bleak conclusion that the bracelet would never be reclaimed. It was gone—unquestionably, irretrievably—and when Nicholas finally confessed the fact to the young woman, he knew that she, too, would be gone forever from his life.

With wistful sadness, he recalled the first moment he had seen her opposite him at his counter. How disparagingly he had judged her, noting that she did not come from wealth or station as many of his clients did. He had come to learn since that day that like the jewels of the angel bracelet that she loved, she had a unique and special beauty all her own. How wrong he'd been about her on that first day she appeared; he had been certain she mistook the angel bracelet for a piece of costume jewelry.

Costume jewelry.

He caught his breath. Could it be possible? The chance was slim, but it was the last—the only—possibility he had.

He checked his watch. One-thirty; he would take

his lunch break now, he told a fellow clerk. Slipping from behind his counter, he fought his way against the flow of shoppers to the section that sold faux and less expensive costume jewelry.

Circling the counters hastily, he scanned the imitation gems: garnets that pretended to be rubies; tanzanite that masqueraded as sapphires. He was approaching the last counter when he saw it. It lay curled on a tray of other bracelets, all on sale. Just one end of the bracelet was visible, but what it showed were two small angels, wingtips touching, their gowns made up of many sparkling clear stones that shone like diamonds in the light.

One clerk stood idle. Nicholas called out to catch the man's attention, and asked to see the tray on which the bracelet lay. Taking note of Nicholas's eagerness, the clerk eyed him briefly with suspicion. Nonetheless, he withdrew the tray and placed it on the countertop. Fingers shaking, Nicholas slid the bracelet from beneath the others, and held it in his palm. Staring down, he could not believe his luck.

To the eye the piece was identical to the angel bracelet. Nicholas saw the row of jeweled angels reached from clasp to clasp. Not waiting for change, Nicholas threw down some money on the counter and raced back to Fine Jewelry. There, he lay the costume bracelet on a chamois and applied a solvent that softened bright metallic finishes to the gold plate that outlined the angels' forms. The stones—zirconia, he guessed—he polished till they sparkled with a luster that surprised even him. Finally, after searching through the cabinet, he found another box similar to the one that had held the angel bracelet, and lined it with the same luxurious blue quilted velvet.

He was about to place the box and bracelet on the top shelf of the display case when a thought occurred to him. He closed the box, slipped from behind the counter, and headed toward the wrapping desk.

The young woman arrived just as the store was closing that evening. Nicholas was at the far end of the section, and he saw her from a distance; her hands pressed to the countertop, her face bent forward toward the glass.

"Good evening," he said smoothly as he eased in opposite her, a smile on his face.

She met his eyes. "It's not here. I waited until tonight. But I guess the jeweler didn't send it back."

"Oh, but he did," said Nicholas. "I have it here."

"Where?"

Grinning now, he put a hand into his pocket and withdrew a rectangular-shaped package. It was wrapped in red-and-green gift paper and tied with a gold bow.

Still smiling, he asked, "What's your name?"

"Mollie. But why—?"

"Merry Christmas, Mollie." He placed the little gift before her.

"What's this?"

"It's for you."

"For me?"

"Yes. Open it."

She glanced at him uncertainly, then took the package in both hands and began unwrapping it, until the box itself was visible. She set it down and raised the lid. Inside, resplendent on its quilted cushion, was the costume bracelet Nicholas had bought.

"It's beautiful," was all she said.

She seemed afraid to touch it, lest she be awakened from a dream.

Instead, Nicholas picked up the bracelet and held it with one hand. "May I?" he asked her. With his other hand, he lifted her right arm toward him, drew the bracelet up around her wrist, and clasped it tight.

Mollie shook her head. "How could you possibly afford . . . ?"

Nicholas was ready for the question. "When the jeweler brought the angel bracelet back, he said he'd found some imperfections. Tiny ones. Invisible to see, in fact, without a microscope. . . ."

He paused to see if she believed him. Trusting spirit that she was, she obviously did. "You can't imagine how much that reduced the price," he went on confidently. "So knowing you were fond of it—"

"You bought it? You bought it for *me*?"

"Yes."

She moved her lips to speak, but no words came. Rather, she continued gazing at it with the joy Nicholas had come to know and love.

When Mollie spoke at last it was to murmur in confusion, "Thank you." Then in a somewhat stronger voice, she said, "I'd like to ask another question. It's a favor, really."

"Oh?"

"Will you walk home with me tonight?"

"Would I do what?" It was now Nicholas who was confused.

"Walk home with me. The bracelet is so beautiful, and it still must have cost something. I'm afraid to wear it on the street alone." She raised her eyes to his. "And

I'm sure that as a store employee, you'd want to see your merchandise delivered safely."

"I—well—yes. I would be very pleased—to see the bracelet safely home," he said.

A short time later, after the store had closed for business for the night, they walked together to the street. As they stepped onto the sidewalk, Nicholas was seen to take hold of Mollie's hand. When she looked puzzled he explained it was a protective gesture intended to discourage any thief from trying to snatch the bracelet from her wrist.

Complete details of what followed that night are known only to Nicholas and Mollie themselves. Still, there is some fragmentary information based on certain facts that Nicholas confided to a fellow clerk a few days later. The weather had turned colder and windy during the couple's walk that night. When they arrived at Mollie's door, so Nicholas admitted to his friend, she invited him inside to warm himself before returning to his own apartment.

While he relaxed Mollie cooked a simple but delicious dinner for them both. She also lit a candle, which she placed between them on the table. From time to time, as the two dined, she would raise her arm, on which she still wore the bracelet, and hold it toward the candlelight. Each time he observed that she smiled very privately to herself as if savoring some secret that she could not share.

As chance would have it, Nicholas admitted further, he and Mollie dined at her apartment on the second evening, and also on the third. On the day after that, which happened to be Christmas Day, Nicholas took Mollie to a restaurant and later the two walked hand in hand about the town, admiring all the brilliant lights and decorations on display. And at all times Mollie wore the bracelet. Often she thanked Nicholas for buying it. To these repeated declarations of her gratitude, he simply answered he was glad circumstances had permitted him to do so. At no time did he confess to her that the bracelet he had given her was not the real angel bracelet but a clever fake.

Yet it appears Mollie was not entirely forthcoming either. It seems that the fellow clerk to whom Nicholas confided the account of his and Mollie's romance had once worked in Costume Jewelry. He knew the imitation bracelet Nicholas had purchased; and he knew that it contained only ten angels, while the real bracelet held twelve. Perceptive as she'd proved to be, Mollie must have realized this from the moment Nicholas clasped the imitation to her wrist.

In fact, it seems quite possible that what drew Mollie on that first day to Nicholas's counter—and what compelled her to return day after day—was not the angel bracelet she had so admired. Nicholas had been correct when he'd believed that she was not a person driven by material possessions. Splendid as the angel bracelet was, the love she felt was not for any object made of minerals and metal. What Mollie just may have been determined to acquire, and to cherish, was the handsome and good-hearted young man who stood behind the counter where the bracelet lay.

What happened to the real bracelet Nicholas and Mollie never learned. But this much is certain. A week after Christmas, Nicholas once again assisted Mollie in the selection of a piece of jewelry. Between them on the counter was a small black open box. This time, it was not Mollie's right arm but her left that was held out in his direction. And it was not a bracelet Nicholas presented to her as she spread the fingers of her hand.

It was a plain gold ring.

THE
CRYSTAL SILVER
CHINA CLUB

*T*emporary help.

Mr. Philip Wetherhew repeated the words in his head as he walked toward the department store. For a man recently retired, Mr. Wetherhew still had a springy step. What's more, he thoroughly enjoyed the spectacle the city streets provided the pedestrian at Christmastime. On every corner there were recently recruited Santa Clauses swinging hand-held bells that tintinnabulated in the cold clear air. There was the pungent smoke of chestnut vendors' carts; the street musicians playing dissonant duets with taxi horns; on doorways, wreaths and bows and boughs of green; across the hard gray granite faces of the buildings everywhere, the festive mantle of a million tiny lights.

Then Mr. Wetherhew remembered he would have a great deal more time for walking now, or for pursuing almost any personal activity he chose. Until two weeks ago his daily walks had brought him to and from the large, impressive-looking banking institution where he had worked for more than forty years. Regrettably, he'd risen to no higher rank than that of Senior Teller. And he looked the part: thin, wispy hair; small, close-set eyes that peered from behind rimless glasses; and a complexion that had the look and color of church candles. A bachelor, he had always lived alone, yet each day he delighted in the brief though pleasant conversations with the bank customers who stood before his teller's cage.

Now all that had ended. It had ended thirteen days ago to be exact. On that last day, his fellow workers at the bank had given him a modest party, and in token of his many years of service had bestowed on him a pocket calculator in a leather case. He had made a pleasant little speech of gratitude, then had put on his coat and soft brown trilby hat and left the bank for the last time.

The day that followed was as empty, dismal, and bereft of human interchange as any Mr. Wetherhew had ever spent. It also prodded him to begin seeking out another job. Therefore, the next morning he bought a newspaper, and immediately scanned the help wanted columns for employment of any kind.

It was there he saw the advertisement placed by the department store. The job was only for the holidays, ending on the last day of the year. But the ad stated there were openings for salesmen available. He responded to the ad, visited the store, was interviewed, and to his great delight was hired on the spot. Today would be his first day on the job—and Mr. Wetherhew could hardly wait.

Fortunately, the store was not far from the building where he lived. His small apartment was two flights up, above a German bakery, and particularly at this season of the year he loved to smell the stollen and rich, thickly crusted breads the baker made. Still, he'd set out earlier than necessary so as to make a good impression on his new employers.

Speculating on the adventure that awaited him, he began to cross a street when a bus horn shook him from his reverie. He jumped back to the curb to let the traffic pass, and as he did, looked across the street. He realized the building that stood opposite him was the department store itself. It was an impressive structure, certainly, at any season of the year. Yet as the holidays approached, it dressed itself in happy expectation. There were lights, and ornaments and greenery in a variety of forms.

The traffic light blinked green, and he crossed with the others to the broad sidewalk bordering the store. The entrance for employees was at the far end of the block, and as Mr. Wetherhew walked toward it, he admired the huge show windows that had been decorated just last week. The theme this year was Christmases of Yesteryear. In each window was a scene representing a holiday of long ago. What made the windows especially appealing to him were the costumed, animated mannequins that were a part of each display. Admittedly, their movements were mechanical, but their attempt at lifelike gestures enlivened the displays far more than immobile figures ever could.

At the employee entrance, Mr. Wetherhew showed his identification to the guard, and went directly to the section he had been assigned—the one that carried china, silver, and glassware of all sorts. He had been given a position selling china plates. Mr. Wetherhew had already met the four other people—a young man and three women—who, like him, had been hired by the store as temporary help for that department.

The young man was named John Stubbins; a lank, lean fellow in his thirties, with long disjointed arms and legs and an attenuated nose on which his glasses sat at some distance from his face, giving him the look of a bespectacled stork. On John Stubbins's application for employment he had stated that his real occupation was a poet. But he also admitted that his great-grandfather had once honed swords for military officers. He was thus directed to assist in selling silverware.

Of the three women, Mrs. Comstock was the oldest; a plump, pleasant widow close to Mr. Wetherhew's own age, and who, like him, had been hired to sell china. Gloria Hyde was in the undeterminable late-thirties to mid-forties range, although her large blue eyes were often downcast, suggesting life had furnished her with more than her share of unfairness. Like John Stubbins she had been assigned to silver. The last of the three women was Priscilla Proctor. Very early twenties, Mr. Wetherhew assumed. Of the group she was the most forthcoming and ingenuous. Her skin was the color of fine porcelain and her delicate hands seemed constantly in flight. Her laughter, which was frequent, had the quality of a glissando played on tiny bits of glass. The section supervisor must have thought so too, since he designated she would be best suited to the glassware and the crystal pieces the department sold.

Had the training sessions lasted longer, or if they had been assigned to work together in the same subsection, a camaraderie might have been born among the five. But it was not. From that first day of work, they went to their own various corners of the vast department and had little contact with each other, except for brief exchanges on the sales floor itself. Even those who worked together, such as John Stubbins and Gloria Hyde, were generally so occupied in serving customers that they rarely had the opportunity to begin any kind of personal acquaintanceship.

If the five ever found themselves together, it was in the area well off the sales floor where the lockers for employees were kept. Every day when they arrived, they would place their coats and other personal belongings in them, murmur a good-morning, and head off to their posts. Each evening, after the store closed, they would retrieve their coats, hastily exchange good-nights, and leave the store.

Now and then, while in the company of one or more of them, Mr. Wetherhew sought to start a conversation. It was futile. Mostly, Priscilla, John, or Gloria would nod and give only a quick social smile before hurrying away. Mrs. Comstock was more understanding. As she put on her coat and hat, she would respond with such expressions as "Do tell," "How nice," and "My, my—very interesting." Then invariably, she would pick up her purse and tell him that she had to hurry home to feed her cats.

It was December 13, Saint Lucia's Day in Sweden, Mr. Wetherhew informed them all that night, as the five were preparing to depart. He had just begun explaining the significance of that day to Swedish people when Mrs. Comstock gave a little cry.

"It's gone!" the woman gasped, a hand thrust in her open purse.

"What's gone?" Priscilla Proctor asked.

"My wallet!" Mrs. Comstock rummaged anxiously. "It must have happened on the bus." More rummaging. "This morning, as I came to work a young man jostled me. Later, when I checked my purse, the clasp was up."

The purse itself was imitation brown leather, small and worn. Mrs. Comstock placed it on a nearby bench, then sat beside it and resumed her frantic searching, now using both her hands.

The others crowded in around her. John Stubbins sat down on the bench beside her.

"Thieves and pickpockets are particularly busy during the holidays," he said, in helpful confirmation of her fears.

"Maybe it fell out," Gloria Hyde offered. "If you call the bus company, a person might have turned it in."

"But I don't have any money to get home," the woman wailed. Mrs. Comstock appeared close to tears.

Mr. Wetherhew sat down on the other side of her. "Don't worry, my dear," he said reassuringly. "We'll give you money to get home."

At once the others spoke up. "No question." "Certainly." "Of course we will."

Mrs. Comstock took a tissue offered by Priscilla and blew her nose. "I was also going to buy groceries. There's not a thing to feed my cats."

Mr. Wetherhew patted her hand. "We'll give you money for that, too."

Once more, there was agreement all around. Gloria Hyde reached into her own purse and withdrew some dollars, which she pressed into Mrs. Comstock's hand.

When the woman started to protest, Gloria insisted that the same thing had happened to her on a subway, and other passengers, complete strangers, gave money to her then. Meanwhile, Mr. Wetherhew, John Stubbins, and Priscilla Proctor all provided words of sympathy and understanding. And they also reached into their wallets, adding to what Gloria had given.

That evening was the beginning of a bond among the five. The next day, quite by chance they found themselves in the employee lunchroom at precisely the same hour, and sat down together with their trays. Mrs. Comstock happily related, though with some embarrassment, that when she returned home she'd found her wallet sitting on the dresser in her bedroom. She then withdrew the wallet from her purse. She remembered to the penny how much money each one of them had given her, and despite their protestations, she paid back each of them in turn.

On the day that followed, they again took lunch together, chatting amiably about the weather, or some news event of consequence, or simply of a sale they had made that day. And as they gathered and conversed, brief lunch upon brief lunch, a portrait of the life of each of them emerged.

For instance, Mrs. Comstock acknowledged over coffee one day that her widowhood, now in its tenth year, had not been easy. With the rising cost of living, any small pleasures she had once enjoyed were dispensed with—dinners in a restaurant, even visits to the theater she loved so much were put aside. Then a month ago, while scanning the newspaper, she'd seen the ad for temporary help at the department store, and had applied.

Gloria Hyde also admitted that as a single mother with a seven-year-old son, plus an apartment, all maintained by fitful alimony checks, a job was a necessity.

John Stubbins stated that though poverty was the

condition of the poet, unpoetic persons such as the land-lord of his building believed otherwise. Certainly, the job of selling silver was not particularly nourishing to his creative soul. But he had already written one piece he had entitled "Tribute to a Silver-plated Biscuit Box."

For her part, Priscilla Proctor said she had sought out her temporary job not because she needed the income such employment provided, but because she loved bright things.

When Mr. Wetherhew's turn came, he paused, reflecting pensively before he answered them. Yes, the extra money gave him certain modest luxuries his pension from the bank did not allow. He also said he loved the Christmas holidays; he enjoyed the sight of shoppers with their brightly colored packages, and what better place to see them every day than in the department store itself. Then Mr. Wetherhew paused for a second time.

"Also," he said finally, "I felt apart. I was an island in an ocean of humanity upon which no visitor set foot." Now, here, even as a temporary sales clerk, he had the opportunity to mix and talk with people once again. He added that he'd recently struck up an acquaintance with the German baker on the ground floor of his building. But the man spoke little English, and Mr. Wetherhew less German, so their communication was limited at best.

The others nodded, but said nothing for some moments. Then Mrs. Comstock readily allowed that it was not just her financial state that had eroded. What she'd lost almost completely were the friends and the acquaintances she had enjoyed when her husband was alive. Some had died, others had moved far away, and still others, who had been business associates of her late husband, had mumbled their condolences at graveside but had not been heard from since.

Gloria Hyde understood. She, too, had no one in her life close to her own age she could call a friend.

John Stubbins told the others that the poet's life demanded that he keep himself apart from day-to-day distractions. But he admitted also that at times the purity of isolation was most difficult to bear.

Priscilla Proctor, for her part, referred to an unfortunate affiliation with a gentleman that had caused her to withdraw into herself. Even her female acquaintances seemed insincere. With the coming of the New Year, she concluded wistfully, she was desirous of creating what she called "a whole new personal persona" for herself.

But it was left to Mr. Wetherhew to summarize what each of them had said in different ways—each one of them was lonely. And such a feeling ran particularly deep at Christmastime: the time when human fellowship was needed most. "Therefore," he said at last, "I recommend we form a club. We can meet here for lunch, and talk among ourselves, and be—well, friends."

The others readily agreed it was a wonderful idea.

"Then our club should have a name," John Stubbins said. "I suggest the Quintessentials. *Quint* means five in Latin, as you know."

"It sounds poetic to me," Mrs. Comstock told him.

"Too poetic," Gloria Hyde said. "Let's call it the Five Who Meet in the Department Store at Christmastime Club."

"Nothing poetic about that," John Stubbins sneered.

"But we did meet in the Crystal Silver China section of the store," Priscilla said.

Mr. Wetherhew leaned back in his chair. "I have it. How about the Crystal Silver China Club?"

The rest said nothing.

Finally, John Stubbins shrugged. "It scans, at least."

"It's dear," said Mrs. Comstock.

Gloria Hyde smiled for the first time any of them could remember. "Yes. I like it. Yes."

"The Crystal Silver China Club!" Priscilla Proctor clapped her hands and blew a kiss to Mr. Wetherhew. "It's beautiful!"

And so, the Crystal Silver China Club was born.

The first official meeting of the Crystal Silver China Club was held at lunch on the next day. Mr. Wetherhew was unanimously voted president. His first official act was to suggest that no new members be admitted, and the rest concurred. Beyond that there were no formal rules, no secret handshakes, no cabalistic rites. Attendance was not mandatory, since one or more of them might be detained on the sales floor on any given day.

It was exactly one week before Christmas that the idea was suggested. And even then it was done in jest.

"Since we're a club," John Stubbins said, "I move we do as other clubs are doing at this time of year and hold a Christmas party for our membership."

"I second that," said Mrs. Comstock, who had once read *Robert's Rules of Order* and knew parliamentary procedure.

"A Christmas party would be fun!" Priscilla said.

"But when and where?" asked Gloria.

"Here in the lunchroom?" Mrs. Comstock wondered.

"No, no," John said. "This lunchroom is all right for our club meetings. But for an organization as exclusive and unique as ours, we need a place that's special."

Mrs. Comstock mentioned the store restaurant. "Maybe one evening after the store is closed, the management would let us hold it there."

She was answered by a rush of alternative ideas, until Mr. Wetherhew finally raised a spoon and tapped his coffee cup. "Members—members, please."

"I propose," he said, when quiet was restored, "that we entertain ideas for a suitable location. Who else has an idea?"

Priscilla said she loved to picnic in the park in summer; was it possible to do some sort of Christmas picnic if the day was nice? A brief discussion followed, and the idea was rejected: it was too cold, the lunch period too brief to allow them to get to and from the park, and Mrs. Comstock knew her arthritis would be felt. Gloria Hyde suggested that she had a friend who owned a fancy rooftop restaurant—maybe he would let them use a room. But John Stubbins said that regrettably his resources were so limited right now a restaurant meal, whether in a basement or on a rooftop, was a luxury that he could ill afford.

"What about somebody's apartment?" John then volunteered, but quickly added that his own was far too small. Mrs. Comstock offered hers, at which Priscilla shook her head and confessed she had an awful allergy to cats.

"Then let me be the host," said Mr. Wetherhew. He smiled broadly, looking from one person to the next.

"I live in a building very near the store. I have the space. And I do not possess a cat."

With grateful murmurs of assent, his invitation was at once accepted and a date was set. The party would be held the evening of December 23, two nights before Christmas, beginning immediately after work.

"Can we sing carols?" asked Priscilla.

Mr. Wetherhew assured her that they could; the walls of his apartment were the brick-and-plaster kind, and the neighbors on each side of him were deaf. Mrs. Comstock informed them she would bring a set of Christmas place mats she had hand-crocheted herself; Gloria said she would prepare a Christmas turkey; and John Stubbins, now caught up in the spirit, promised he would write a special ode commemorating the occasion, and would read it aloud to the assemblage as the evening's pièce de résistance.

The lunch period ended shortly after that. The five rose from the table with their trays, anticipation showing on the faces of them all. The Christmas party of the Crystal Silver China Club would be the finest ever held, they all agreed.

In the days that followed, the lunch periods they shared were filled with planning and a sense of growing expectation. They made a list of what dishes they would serve. To accompany the turkey Gloria had volunteered to roast, Priscilla offered to bring biscuits and tomato timbales. Mrs. Comstock would contribute green beans and pearl onions in a flavored cream sauce, prepared according to an honored family recipe. Mr. Wetherhew insisted on providing the hors d'oeuvres—spiced walnuts, buttery almonds, and a variety of cheeses, hard and soft. As an added treat, he said he'd found a bottle of champagne in his closet that had been given to him years ago for an occasion he could not recall. In the intervening years he'd had no reason to enjoy it alone. Their party would provide a splendid opportunity to share it. The only item that the five agreed to purchase was a special fruitcake sold exclusively by the Food and Gourmet section of the store. Priscilla and John both confessed they'd nibbled samples of it, and it was by far the best they'd ever had.

But obstacles arose as well. Where, they wondered, would they keep the food before the party, if they went directly from the store to Mr. Wetherhew's? Gloria told them she was having difficulty locating a baby-sitter for her son that evening. And when asked about the poem he had promised to recite in honor of the party, John admitted that his muse had been a coy mistress; he had written several versions of the initial strophe, and was dissatisfied with the results.

Yet somehow by the morning of December 23, whatever impediments existed earlier were overcome. Priscilla had made the acquaintance of the young manager of a pizza parlor opposite the store, and he had agreed to let them store their food in his refrigerators for the day. Gloria had obtained a sitter for her son. And John in exultation had at last been embraced fully by the capricious muse. ("Hark! Hark! We five who sit before this holiday repast . . ." he told them it began.)

Mr. Wetherhew apologized that his table settings would be no match for the elegant pieces they themselves sold in the department store: his plates, cups, and saucers were of simple ironstone; the utensils, stainless steel; and the glassware an assortment of odd pieces Mr. Wetherhew had had for years. But no one seemed to mind. They were friends, now, each one of them said in different ways, and the pleasure they would share in one another's company was what delighted them the most.

At last, the evening arrived. The group had pre-arranged that Mr. Wetherhew would go directly to his apartment and await them there. Priscilla, John, and Gloria were to go across the street to the pizza parlor where their food was being kept, retrieve it, and return to the employees' entrance of the store, where Mrs. Comstock waited. Then, John would go out on the street once more, and wave down a taxi that would take the four of them to Mr. Wetherhew's apartment.

Thus, when the closing hour came, they all headed toward the lockers where their coats were kept. Mr. Wetherhew put on his coat and scarf. He donned his trilby, tapped the brim in jaunty fashion, and departed. The other four put on their coats as well and left. Less than five minutes after that, Priscilla, John, and Gloria returned with shopping bags of food, to rejoin Mrs. Comstock, who waited by the door.

John set down the shopping bag he carried. "Stay here," he advised the women. "I'll find a cab and we'll be off."

He stepped onto the sidewalk—and was stopped abruptly by the specter that he saw. Moving slowly down the sidewalk came a man who was the picture of despair. His coat was covered with powdery gray soot. His hat was blackened at the crown. Black smudges like-wise covered the man's face and hands.

The man was Mr. Wetherhew. "There's been a fire," he said simply, as the others gaped.

As soon as he had stepped inside the door, he endeavored to explain. He said that as he'd hurried home to prepare for their arrival, the sound of fire sirens could be heard. The nearer he came to his own block the louder the wail of the sirens was. Turning the corner, finally, he saw fire engines parked from curb to curb, their twirling dome lights thrusting crimson streaks into the night. The fire that still burned was in the bakeshop of the building where he lived. The German baker, rushing to fill Christmas orders, apparently had let an oven overheat.

The blaze itself was contained within the bakery, Mr. Wetherhew went on. The upper stories of the building were untouched by flames. But smoke and water damage had rendered three apartments uninhabitable. He added, "Mine was one."

There were immediate expressions of concern and sympathy. As to his well-being, Mr. Wetherhew was grateful to some neighbors who had invited him to stay with them until his own place was restored. Still, he confirmed what the others knew but did not say. The Christmas party they had planned so carefully was not to be.

"Can't we postpone it till another time?" Priscilla asked.

"But we have all the food right here," said Gloria.

"And it's two days to Christmas," John told them. "After that, it wouldn't be the same."

Mrs. Comstock shook her head. She just wished there was someplace in the store itself where they could hold the party, since it was here the five of them had met and become friends.

The others shook their heads as well—except for the club president, who smiled suddenly.

"Perhaps there is," said Mr. Wetherhew. He was recalling the first morning he had come to work. He remembered walking past the display windows with their animated figures, all depicting Christmases of long ago.

"Perhaps there is," he said again, and went on smiling as he brushed some cinders from his hat.

Throughout the day of December 24, spokespersons for the department store disclaimed all knowledge of the incident. *Baffled* was the word they used. The first call was received shortly before midnight by the Shoppers' Hotline, an 800 number that the store maintained, and whose operators answered round-the-clock. The operator who wrote down the information was convinced the caller had imbibed excessively of Christmas cheer. But as the calls continued through the night and into the next morning, store officials were informed. All those who telephoned, the operators said, were complimentary. The display windows were always a delight at Christmastime, the callers told them, but the tableau they enjoyed most was the one in window number 17.

By noon so many calls had come to the department store that two members of the management, the decorator who had dressed the windows, and a security guard went together to examine window 17. They entered from a rear door, drew down the shadelike covering that prevented passersby from looking in, and carefully examined the display.

The scene was an elegant Victorian dining room. The paneling was of walnut, burnished to a deep rich luster, against which sconces gleamed. Above, a crystal chandelier appeared to glitter with a thousand lights. Beneath it was an elaborately carved oak table. Covering the table was a damask linen tablecloth on which five table settings had been placed. Each setting was a work of art—the finest china, crystal stemware, and a silver service, each piece of which was engraved with a design of exquisite detail. A pair of crystal candlelabras at each end of the table also lit the faces of the dinner guests—an older man and woman, two younger women, and a young man. They were dressed in costumes of the period; the men in waistcoats, and the women in long dresses with lace ruffles at their throats. And all five mannequins appeared to be enjoying a splendid Christmas feast.

The department store was noted for the animated mannequins the decorators placed in the show windows during the holidays. Though composed of plastic and epoxy in their major parts, the faces and joints of the mannequins contained a pliable rubberized material which, when the mannequins were connected to their power source, made them appear to move and talk, and even eat, as naturally as real human beings would. But what the callers to the store remarked on was the particularly lively spirit of the figures in window 17. Several of the callers went on to insist that they had heard them singing Christmas carols, something store officials knew the mannequins were not equipped to do.

Despite a brief but diligent investigation, the store

employees found nothing in window 17 that could have precipitated such a strange response. All was just as it should be. The five mannequins turned their heads, raised forks and glasses to their lips, and seemed to speak to one another as they always had since they were placed there several weeks before. Satisfied that nothing was amiss, the store employees drew up the window covering and exited from the display.

Still, calls continued though the afternoon, and that evening two guards from the night security detail were assigned to watch the window; one stationed near the rear door, the other on the street outside. For eight hours they watched window 17. They had absolutely nothing to report.

A week later, December 31, the coverings of all the display windows were drawn down; the scenes of Christmases of Yesteryear were disassembled, and the mannequins removed, in order to make way for displays featuring cruisewear and the annual white sale. A member of the cleaning staff vacuuming the floor of window 17 later in the day was briefly puzzled to discover a champagne cork lying in a corner. He put it in his pocket, and afterward he tossed the cork into the trash.

On that last day of the year also, temporary store employees who had been hired for the holiday shopping season were released by the department store with great appreciation for the work they'd done. Among those dismissed were five temporary salespeople from the Crystal Silver China section of the store, who in the few weeks they had worked together appeared to have become great friends.

The so-called mystery of window 17 was never solved. Store officials finally concluded that the Christmas party many claimed they witnessed was a product of the callers' own imaginations, and that the feelings of festivity and fellowship they swore they saw among the mannequins in window 17 were an illusion, stimulated by the spirit of the holiday itself.

EAU DE NOEL

*T*hey were the best of friends. If there was a
female equivalent of Castor and Pollux, Damon and
Pythias, David and Jonathan, it would be Evaline and
Rose. Several of their neighbors in the apartment building where they lived called them the Two Musketeers, so
inseparable did they appear. Each woman had her own
small studio apartment, side-by-side in the old Beaux
Arts–style building that had once been a residence for
genteel working women. Evaline had lived there thirty
years; Rose just under ten.

Both women were in their middle sixties. Both were
retired; Evaline from an accounting firm where she had
been the office manager. Rose had been assistant book-
keeper for a manufacturer of twine. Both lived on modest pensions. Evaline also received occasional cash gifts
from an aged uncle, who was her only living relative.

Rose, on the other hand, had no one. Neither woman had married, although Rose had been affianced to a young man who had died tragically as the result of bee stings while picking wildflowers for her in the park.

In physical appearance Evaline and Rose were not at all alike. At just under five feet, Evaline was a good ten inches shorter than her friend. She was also heavier by fifty pounds, which a variety of firm foundation garments could not hide. Her face was flat, accentuated by an upturned and truncated nose; Rose's face, in contrast, was angular, with high cheekbones and a delicately sculpted nose above which large brown eyes looked somewhat wistfully upon the world. Both women had gray hair cut straight around their heads, although in public Evaline enveloped hers with an enormous black felt hat.

Still, whatever differences there were, the women's lives were intertwined—their similarities in age and social circumstance, the proximity of their apartments, and a simple human longing for companionship. They ate dinners together, generally at a tearoom in the neighborhood; shared the same newspaper (Evaline made sure it was delivered to her doorstep first); and attended concerts and museums in each other's company. On Evaline's insistence the two also did their Christmas shopping in October; mostly, though, the only gifts they bought were for each other, and then always of the utilitarian, nonfrivolous variety: dish towels, tea cozies, decorated dustpans, and the like.

What brought them to the department store in the middle of December several years ago was an untoward incident that had happened to Evaline the day before. As Evaline was heading homeward from the grocery store, she had stumbled on a piece of broken pavement, fallen, and in so doing, badly scuffed the leather of both shoes. The shoes were made of cowhide, solid black with rounded toes, flat rubber heels, and wide black shoelaces with plastic tips. In sum, footwear that bespoke practicality and durability. Thus Evaline had no other recourse, she informed Rose, than to visit the department store and purchase a new pair.

Evaline had next pointed to the shoes Rose herself was wearing, and suggested bluntly that her friend could also do with a new pair. Rose, whose shoes were similar to Evaline's, had bought them just last spring and saw no need for new ones. But to please her, Rose agreed.

"We won't make any other purchases," Evaline had stated. "We will arrive at the department store as the doors are being opened. We will go directly to the section that sells ladies' shoes, select ours, and depart."

"If that's what you want, Evaline," her friend had said.

It was.

The next morning the two women left their apartment building early, bound for the department store. They arrived at the precise hour that the big doors were being unlocked for the day.

As the guards began to do so, Evaline adjusted her hat, lowered her head, and aimed herself in the direction of the doors like a missile ready to be launched. The moment passage through them was assured, Evaline shot forward. Several steps behind, Rose followed in her wake.

To the surprise of both women, there were already a few shoppers in the aisles, presumably from other doors that had been opened earlier. Evaline halted and frowned briefly. Then she turned her body sideways so as to align herself with an adjacent aisle, readjusted her hat, and propelled her short, squat body down the aisle with resolve.

What Evaline, with her head lowered, didn't notice—and Rose did—was that the aisle along which they were bound led through the Cosmetics section of the store. In the days preceding Christmas, Cosmetics was particularly busy. Generally, whatever male customers there were made speedy purchases and fled. It was the women, on the other hand, who lingered, sampling the perfumes and the powders, sniffing vials of cologne and toilet water, and gazing into mirrors at their own expectant faces that would soon be metamorphosed by the miracle of cosmetology.

"Eau de Noel!"

"Eau de Noel!"

Ahead of them, on both sides of the aisle, were a half dozen pert young women wearing jumpers trimmed in red and green and holding atomizers in their hands.

"Eau de Noel!" the young women chirped at passersby. "Take a moment, ladies! Try our special holiday perfume!"

It was then Rose saw a small sign that had been placed on the countertop nearby. The sign read:

EAU DE NOEL
Sample our new holiday perfume. Experience the essence of this joyous season that promises a joyous new
YOU!

"May I spray a bit on both you ladies?" one of the young women asked of Evaline and Rose.

"No," said Evaline at once. Before Rose could respond, Evaline had seized her arm and started toward another aisle.

Evaline had taken only three steps when it happened. Head down and moving at determined speed, she ran squarely into a lone woman with an atomizer in her hand. At once, the young woman's hand flew up, the atomizer fired, and a scented mist was sprayed on Evaline's hat and Rose's face.

"What on earth—" Evaline stopped and glared at the offender.

"I'm terribly sorry," the young woman apologized. She took a box of tissues from the counter next to them and wiped vigorously at Evaline's hat. She continued murmuring apologies, while Evaline removed the hat and fussed.

For her part, Rose was totally ignored. Blinded momentarily, she opened the purse she had been carrying, felt around, and finally found a tissue she could use. Keeping her eyes closed, she patted them. At last she opened them, anticipating that her sight would be restored. It was, but very indistinctly. When she looked down the aisle, all she could make out was a fuzzy round form of Evaline proceding at a rapid pace. Evaline was on the march toward Ladies' Shoes once more, unmindful of her friend.

Rose took a breath and started after her. But she had only gone three steps before she felt disoriented, stopped, and clutched the counter for support. Whatever properties that perfume had, they still affected her. Her vision swam, her legs felt weak, her heartbeat echoed in her ears. She wondered briefly if the perfume had contained some chemical ingredient to which she was allergic.

Again she closed her eyes. What was the perfume's scent? Lilac? Oleander? Jasmine with a hint of holly leaves? Whatever essence it might be, it was extraordinarily pleasant, although Rose didn't value her ability to judge. Evaline believed that perfumes led to exploitation of a woman's vanity, and out of deference to her, Rose wore none. Indeed, not a drop of perfume had touched Rose's body since the last opportunity for romance had faded from her life.

Maybe that was the reason Rose was feeling so peculiar now. Quite literally, it took her breath away. As with the first alcoholic spirits she had tasted—the may wine her grandmother had served to her at the age of twelve—Rose suddenly felt giddy with delight. If what she was experiencing was the perfume, it brought about the most appealing, most remarkable sensation Rose had ever known.

The moment Evaline arrived in Ladies' Shoes, she knew exactly where the shoes she wanted could be found. She marched directly to the shelf, grabbed a box, and read the information printed on the end. Then, clutching the box with one hand, she removed the lid, pawed apart the tissue paper, and removed the shoes.

She held one aloft, appraising it. "They haven't changed a bit," she said. "I'm sure they have a pair in your size, Rose," she added, turning.

Rose was nowhere to be seen.

Rose bent closer to the tray of watches that the sales-clerk had set out on the countertop. By blinking rapidly and concentrating hard she found her focus was becoming more distinct: no longer did the faces of the watches float before her eyes like golden disks.

"Are you all right?" the clerk inquired.

Rose straightened. She blinked at the man twice. "I'm fine," she said. "In fact, I'm very fine." She thanked him for the time he'd showed her, laughed a bit too loudly at her unintended pun, and stepped away.

Standing in the middle of the aisle, she suddenly felt herself bumped from behind. She turned to find that she was looking up at the thin face of a tall man in a blue overcoat, carrying a shopping bag.

"Please do excuse me," the man hastened to say.

"It was my fault," Rose said at once. "I was standing in the aisle." She looked down at her feet. "I still am, actually," she told him, and retreated to the side.

"Even so, I do apologize," the man insisted. He gave her a quick smile and rejoined the still-moving crowd.

Rose leaned against the edge of the counter nearest her and let the customers flow past while she decided what to do. Already there were many people in the store. But where was Evaline? Rose guessed her friend had found her way to Ladies' Shoes and was seated in a chair, one bare foot perched on a stool, while she waved a shoehorn in the air and yoo-hooed to attract attention from the sales help. Evaline was probably also practicing her statements of displeasure, which she would direct at Rose when the two met.

Rose looked around. Now slowly she began to walk the aisle, lightly touching the counter for support. She had gone only a short distance, however, when she realized that she had absolutely no idea where the Ladies' Shoe department was. Rose paused, pursed her lips, and thought. Whenever she and Evaline had visited the store, they'd gone directly to the sections Evaline had chosen for them. And each time Evaline had led the way. Rose considered looking for an information desk or store directory. But until the effects of the perfume had worn off further, she decided not to rush. Instead, she would move at an unhurried pace, perhaps browsing now and then to see what special Christmas items the department store displayed. If her wanderings turned out to be circuitous and leisurely, Rose thought, her friend would simply have to understand.

So following no predetermined route, Rose set forth again among the crowds of customers. She visited departments as diverse as Clocks and Intimates, Books and Bedding, Leather Goods and Lamps. In Handbags, she discovered a luxurious suede purse in beige that bore a monogrammed gold *R* above the clasp. In Dance and Exercise Apparel, she smiled at envisioning herself in purple leotards practicing jetés. In Gourmet Foods, she bought a little decorated box of Christmas toffees and commenced to sample them as she continued on.

It was as Rose was on her way to Soaps and Sachets that the tall man with the shopping bag appeared once more.

"Ah, what a remarkable coincidence," he told her,

as he stepped out before her in the aisle. "Of all these people in the store, we two have met again. But this time maybe you can help me." Looking at him as he spoke, Rose saw that he was in his sixties, with gray hair and a small gray mustache. The shopping bag he carried bore the name and emblem of the department store, and it was filled with wrapped, beribboned boxes.

"I don't know," she said. "I'll try."

"As you can see," he said, pointing at the bag, "I've done a good amount of shopping here today. But for the life of me, I can't remember where women's scarves are sold."

Rose shook her head. "I—really hardly know the store myself."

"I see. Well, I'm quite sure I'll find it. Thank you anyway." He nodded pleasantly and turned away—then caught himself, and turned back. "Please, one final question, if I may. That delightful perfume that you're wearing—does it have a name?"

The comment caught her by surprise. "I don't—I'm not certain. I think Eau de Noel. That's the name."

"Enchanting," the man said. "Like the wearer." He inclined his head in her direction, smiled, and went on his way.

Rose watched him go. When he was finally out of sight, she closed her eyes and drew another long deep breath. By now, the fragrance had faded somewhat. But after two brief chance encounters in the store, a man, a perfect stranger she had never seen before, had complimented her because of it.

"Eau de Noel," she repeated to herself. "Eau de Noel."

In Millinery, Rose tried on several hats, but was particularly taken with a claret-colored beret, which she modeled at a rakish angle on her head.

At Bridal Registry, she gazed with just a touch of longing at the exquisitely styled trousseaus with their yards of tulle, pearls, and fine lace.

In Hosiery, she lingered longer than she ever would have in the past considering a pair of crimson leggings. On them was a design of tiny butterflies that fluttered from the ankles to the calves. Certainly, the nature of her own life had never encouraged Rose to wear anything so daring. But as she held them up, it pleased her suddenly to realize for the first time that possibly her life *could* change, and that like butterflies, she too could shed the chrysalis that had enclosed her for so long.

From Hosiery, Rose went on to Umbrellas. The lone umbrella that she owned was a very large black model that Evaline had given her six Christmases before. The fabric had become separated from the struts in places, and the catch was loose, which caused it to fold up at the most inconvenient times. Rose decided she would buy a new one for herself.

Spring was still more than three months away, but she chose a pale yellow umbrella with white daisies encircling the edge. After inspecting it, she turned it sideways to unfold it. And stopped. Three aisles over, a man stood with his back to her. One hand held an open umbrella over his shoulder, so that Rose couldn't see his face, or even the back of his head. But what she saw was that he was tall, his overcoat was blue, and in his other hand he gripped a shopping bag.

The man was following her! The more Rose thought of it the more convinced she was. Perhaps even their second meeting hadn't been all that "coincidental" after all. Yet to her considerable surprise, the possibility aroused in her no sense of fear. He had been well dressed and gracious: not the type to do a person harm. Indeed, he seemed the sort of man whose very mystery intrigued her. And, Rose admitted to herself, she was intrigued.

When a salesclerk approached, Rose ordered the umbrella with the daisies to be sent. She left the section quickly, glancing cautiously around her as she did. At the far end of the floor was the department that sold picture frames and mirrors, and she headed toward it. On a table near the entrance was a variety of small hand-held mirrors, suitable for a woman's dressing table or toilette. Some had gilded handles, others were of wood, and still others were inlaid with inexpensive gems. She selected one set inside a fruitwood frame.

But, lifting it to look at her reflection, Rose saw something else. Behind her, no more than fifteen feet away, half hidden by a standing panel on which picture frames were hung, she saw him. This time there was no doubt of who it was. She set the mirror down at once and turned to face him. But by then the man had disappeared.

A tremor radiated through her. But as before it was not fear but puzzlement and a strange thrill she felt.

She took the mirror in her hand again, and looked at it. The face she saw now was as readable as year-old newsprint—and as interesting. Rose knew exactly what her next stop in the department store would be.

"*Les oeils*—the eyes, . . . *Trés belle, oui?*" asked the girl hovering beside her. Rose sat, half reclining, in a vast white leather armchair in the Beauty Center of the store. The eyes that now stared back at her from the mirrored wall blinked simultaneously with Rose's own. But the eyeliner, mascara, and eye shadow the cosmetician had applied made them barely recognizable. The hair, now gently waved and styled, was a tawny red. It matched the color nail polish that the manicurist had brushed on.

Rose lifted one hand to study it, then raised the hand still farther so as to touch her face. The woman in the mirror did the same. The face shone soft and supple from the creams that had been massaged onto it; the deep red lips glowed beckoningly from the glass.

Now, very slowly, those lips of the woman in the mirror parted in a smile.

"*Oui,*" said Rose. "*Trés belle.*"

The first elevator to arrive was jammed with shoppers; Rose had been about to enter it, but stepped back when she saw the crowd. When the doors had closed, she scanned the store directory posted on the wall nearby, and discovered there was a café restaurant on the same floor. She decided that a cup of coffee and a sweet bun might taste good.

The restaurant was a short walk from the elevators. Most of the small tables were open to the floor itself, though separated from it by a metal railing. Rose found an empty table with two chairs and sat down. The tabletops were round and made of marble; the chairs were wire frame, with the backs shaped so as to form a heart. The tables and chairs reminded Rose of the ice cream parlor she had visited so often as a child. Always she would ask to have her favorite—the Rainbow Medley parfait, a tall wide glass with a variety of ice creams: lemon, raspberry, pistachio, and strawberry among them, whose colors she could swirl in great loops and whorls as she stirred the spoon. How long ago that was. How many years had passed since there'd been any real color in her life at all.

Today, however, she had visited this wonderful department store. By accident a perfume had been sprayed into her eyes, and for a brief time after that her vision had been blurred. But once restored, she'd seen the world with a brightness and a clarity she'd never known.

Eau de Noel—Water of Christmas—the manufacturer had called it. What a silly name that was. And yet the fragrance of it had been intriguing, and Rose was rather sorry it had faded, to be replaced by the exotic scents of the emollients, creams, and sprays the Beauty Center people had applied. Rose decided she would buy a little bottle of it on her way out of the store, as a memento of the day she'd spent. She also smiled to herself, remembering the small sign on the counter in Cosmetics that had advertised "a joyous new YOU!"

"Hello," a voice said.

Rose turned. The tall man with the shopping bag was standing at her table facing her.

He gestured to the empty chair. "Are you expecting someone?"

"No."

"Then may I join you?"

Rose nodded. The man smiled, set the shopping bag down on the floor between them, and sat opposite her. He raised his head and looked at her, but did not speak. He simply stared.

Flustered, Rose said, "You seem to have done quite a bit of shopping." She glanced down at the bag of gifts.

"Yes," he said. "They're for my wife."

It was not the answer Rose had been prepared for.

"Oh," was all she said.

A waitress now appeared beside the table. Rose quickly checked the menu card, and realized she had no appetite.

"Would you like something?" the man asked her.

"No." Rose shook her head. "Perhaps just tea."

"Something more?"

"No, thank you."

The man looked up at the waitress. "Make that two teas, if you please."

The woman wrote the information on the pad and went away. Avoiding his eyes, Rose watched her go. When they were alone again, the man leaned across the table and stretched out a hand. "At first, I didn't recognize you sitting here." He made a wavy motion with his hand above his head. "Your hair—"

"I had it done."

"It's most becoming."

"Thank you."

Several tables from them two women in their early twenties, also with fresh coiffures, giggled over some shared confidence. The man inclined his head in their direction.

"I've often thought," he said, "that certain women

expect beauty treatments to create another self, a new and different one from what they are."

He fixed his eyes on Rose. "But other women, wiser women, know such treatments reawake the beauty that exists within. That's one reason I find women of mature years far more interesting than younger ones. They know the loveliness that is inside them, and have nurtured it the way they would a flower waiting to burst forth. To quote the poet: 'More exquisite than any other is the autumn rose.' "

"My name is Rose."

"It is?" He leaned back in his chair, amused. "You see? I must have known."

Their tea arrived. The waitress set the cups and saucers down and asked if either of them cared for something more. The man said no. Rose shook her head.

When the waitress had gone the man turned to Rose and once more reached a hand in her direction. Then, reconsidering, he placed the hand around the cup, so that his fingers touched the lip.

"I owe you an apology," he said to Rose.

"Oh?"

"Yes." He raised his hand and wiped the lower edge of his mustache, as if uncertain what he should say next.

At last, he gestured toward the shopping bag. "I mentioned to you that I bought these presents for my wife. Every year at Christmastime since we were married, I've gone to one store or another buying gifts for her."

"I don't—"

"Let me explain. She passed away this year. Not long ago. Even so, I came here to the store today and bought the gifts I knew she would have liked: scarves, jewelry, gloves—she particularly loved French kid gloves. I know it seems a sad, even a pathetic thing to do. But perhaps it was my way of softening my grief, a way to keep her memory alive."

Rose started to speak again but he spoke first. "Then quite by accident I saw you in the store today. I confess, you—shall we say, you bear a great resemblance to her. So much so that I followed you from one department to another." He gave Rose a small smile. "I told you I almost didn't recognize you when you came out of the Beauty Center. And I was glad you didn't take that first elevator that arrived."

He reached down, raised the shopping bag with both hands, and placed it on the table. "Now," he said, "if it is not too presumptuous of me to suggest it, I would like to give these gifts to you."

"What? Here? Oh no—I couldn't possibly—"

"Not here." His smile broadened. "Shall we say tonight at dinner? There's a splendid little restaurant I can recommend." He pulled a business card out of his pocket and wrote quickly on the other side, then held up the card for her to see. "This is the restaurant. . . ." He turned the card around. "And this is my name."

Rose took the card and looked at it. "I don't know what to say."

"A simple yes will do. Shall we say eight o'clock? Oh, and another thing. I did buy one gift especially for you." He put a hand into the shopping bag and lifted out a small rectangular-shaped box, which he put down before her.

Rose looked at the box tentatively. "What is it?" she asked.

"Open it and see."

She raised the lid. Inside was a small vial of perfume. The label read "Eau de Noel."

By all accounts Rose and her friend Evaline were never seen together in the department store again. Members of the sales staff, however, did acknowledge sightings of a short round woman in a felt hat who annually bought black cowhide shoes. The woman was alone.

Reports from many other sections, nonetheless, confirm the visits of an auburn-haired woman in her sixties, accompanied by a tall man with a mustache. Often they walk arm-in-arm. But what is most evident about the couple is their obvious delight in one another's company, and in the woman's case, the *joie de vivre* that she displays. She is particularly fond, it seems, of browsing here and there in the Cosmetics section of the store.

As for the fragrance—Eau de Noel—that had been featured before Christmas, it was discontinued soon after the holiday. Instead, the formula was altered slightly, and the perfume was rebottled and relabeled under the new name of Winter Whispers. To encourage customers to sample it, the demonstrator girls no longer dressed in red-and-green attire, but rather wore short all-white outfits, with glass earrings in the shape of icicles that dangled from their ears.

Another change that happened in Cosmetics after Christmas that year is worth noting. In the aisles adjacent to where the demonstrator girls stood, a woman formerly appeared every morning with an atomizer in her hand. The woman was employed by the maintenance department of the store. It was her job to moisten the many potted flowers the store's decorators had set out. Now, another woman mists the plants and flowers in the evening after all the customers have gone.

This alteration in procedure was made necessary by a pre-Christmas incident. As the morning maintenance woman had been spraying the flowers, a female shopper had bumped into her; the atomizer accidentally discharged, and in so doing sprayed the shopper and another woman just behind. No complaint was ever lodged with the department store, although the second shopper seemed disoriented briefly, probably from surprise. In any case, there was nothing in the contents of the atomizer to cause lasting harm. The liquid was no more than common tap water with a few drops of cologne added to provide a pleasant scent.

LOST
AND
FOUND

$\mathcal{Y}$ou found it! Bless you!" said the woman. She was staring at the tiny gold-plated head of cabbage Jonathan held in his hand.

"It fitted the description," Jonathan said. "Perhaps if you could—"

"Yes yes. It's mine, all right. Here's the mate."

The woman hefted her huge purse onto the desk and opened it. She plunged both arms inside, and after a short time in which all sides of the purse bulged briefly from her rummaging, she withdrew an earring identical to the one Jonathan held. It, too, was a miniature gold-plated cabbage head.

"My husband's gift to me on our first anniversary," the woman said. "He's a grocery man, and I was shopping for a cabbage when we met. He picked one out for me. Then he picked *me*."

She gave a little laugh.

"We're glad to be of help," Jonathan told her, and released the single earring to her custody.

The woman dropped both earrings into her purse, thanked him extravagantly, and hurried from the Lost and Found department of the store. Jonathan picked up the ledger the department maintained, and after the entry reading "Lost—Dec. 18—One cabbage earring, gold-plated," he wrote "Found and returned to owner—Dec. 19." He thought of adding that it was the ugliest pair of earrings he had ever seen.

His full name was Jonathan James Jessup. He was in his middle thirties. His two front teeth slightly over-lapped his lower lip. But that fact was only noticeable when he smiled broadly, and moments such as those were rare. He wore tortoiseshell-frame glasses and a dark blue suit and tie. He was of average height and weight. Indeed, there was a great deal about Jonathan James Jessup that was average.

Even so, he was the senior clerk of Lost and Found. Otherwise, the staff consisted of Miss Brophy, a mousy woman about Jonathan's own age, who nevertheless called him "sir"; and Felix, a jaunty fellow in his twenties, who snapped gum out of the corner of his mouth while talking, and wore his trouser cuffs an inch too short.

What had earned Jonathan his position as the head of the department was an extraordinary talent that his colleagues did not share. It was his unerring ability to reunite concerned and sometimes desperate shoppers with the objects they had lost within the store. At the mere sight of a man or woman coming through the door, Jonathan seemed able to divine precisely what article that person had misplaced. The incident two days ago was an example. A portly man had trundled toward his desk in an excited manner. Before the man could speak, Jonathan knew intuitively that the man had lost a black umbrella. At all times of the year Lost and Found was the repository of numerous umbrellas, many of them black. But in his fleeting study of the man, Jonathan correctly guessed which of the several dozen black umbrellas lying on the shelf was his.

Still, there was one loss Jonathan believed was irretrievable. His failure to restore it to its owner was all the more acute because the man came to the Lost and Found department every day wishing it could somehow be reclaimed. The man was Jonathan himself. What he had lost was not a tie clip, or a glove, or a personalized handkerchief. It was not an object to be placed among the other unclaimed items on the shelves.

What Jonathan had lost was hope.

His loss was such that earlier that morning, before the other members of the staff appeared, he had gone so far as to take a copy of the printed claim form used by Lost and Found and fill it out. On the lines listing the name and address of the claimant Jonathan had put his own. In that portion of the form asking him to state the item lost, he had printed the word in large block letters—H-O-P-E. As for the specific color, shape, and dimensions of the article in question, Jonathan left those lines blank.

On the other hand, to simply write that he had lost his hope seemed insufficient to describe the malaise of the spirit that had overcome him in the last few years. No more was there the optimism and the buoyancy of youth. No more did he retain his sense of trust and confidence in humankind, nor the certainty that he would ever find fulfillment in his life. As a child he had clung to the belief that in some unexpected ways his life would become bountiful and blessed. But it had not.

Now, the Christmas holidays were drawing near: that time of year when all the world seemed to overflow with warmth and jollity and love. Jonathan felt none of these. Everywhere he looked there were the bright and festive colors of the season. But refracted through the prism of his spirit, they were little more than somber shades of gray.

After Jonathan had signed his own name at the bottom of the claim form, this time as department representative, and had stamped the date—December 19—he was about to add it to those already in the file. But on the chance the other clerks might come across it, he tore it up and threw the pieces in the trash.

It was about five-thirty that same evening when the datebook was turned in by a store clerk from the Men's Apparel section of the store. It had been found lying in a changing booth, according to the clerk. As Jonathan did every year in the weeks preceding Christmas, he had been working well past closing time to catalog the dozens of stray articles that poured into the Lost and Found at that time of year. He had already examined thirteen single gloves. There were also a variety of ladies' compacts; two leather briefcases; several hats, both men's and women's; and a pocket humidor with one slightly chewed cigar.

But it was the datebook that caught Jonathan's particular attention. It was small—pocket-size, in fact—and bound in dark brown leather. A gold monogram *J* had been imprinted on the front. Jonathan remembered seeing similar datebooks in the Stationery section of the store. He had even considered purchasing one for himself, until he realized that he had nothing to look forward to this year or next.

He opened the datebook hoping he would find the owner's name, address, or phone. But no such information was in evidence.

He put down the datebook and consulted the claim forms filled out by prospective claimants for that day. A brown leather datebook with a *J* was not mentioned among them. He checked the forms for every day of the preceding week. Still nothing. He considered looking back still further to the week before that, but it was late and he was tired. Instead, he decided to go home.

Perhaps it was the lateness of the hour, perhaps it was fatigue or mere forgetfulness. But what Jonathan did next was contrary to his methodic nature. Rather than place the datebook on the shelves with the other unclaimed articles, he absentmindedly dropped it into the inner pocket of his suit jacket where his eyeglasses were kept. Soon after that he left the store.

A short time later, Jonathan entered the narrow foyer of the brownstone apartment building where he lived. He collected the day's mail from the row of mailboxes in the wall, unlocked another door, and began walking slowly up the creaking stairway to his own small apartment on the topmost floor. Once inside, he hung his overcoat and suit jacket in the closet, sat down in the single armchair that he owned, and began riffling through the accumulated mail. There were three pleas for help from a variety of charities, all voicing their standard holiday appeals. These Jonathan discarded in a wastebasket that sat near his chair.

There was also what appeared to be a Christmas card, addressed to him in a spidery, uncertain hand. Inside it was a check for twenty dollars; as it had been for many years now, the accustomed Christmas present from an aged aunt. Knowing he would need his glasses to read the note she had attached, Jonathan went to the closet where his suit jacket had been hung, and reached into the inside pocket. To his surprise, his hand withdrew not only his glasses but also the little datebook he had come across that evening in the store. His first impulse was to return the book to his pocket, and in the morning take it back to Lost and Found. Yet as he studied it, his curiosity increased. The gold *J* printed on the datebook's cover was probably the first letter of the owner's name. But it could also stand for Jonathan, or Jessup, or for that matter, his own middle name of James.

Jonathan carried his glasses and the datebook to the armchair and sat down again. He put aside his aunt's card and opened the datebook. This time he was aware of something he had not noticed earlier. Although the datebook had originally contained pages for an entire year—a page for every date—the ones prior to today had been torn out. The pages that remained held entries only for the last days of the year.

The page with today's date—December 19—was empty. Jonathan turned to the next day, December 20. In a bold and definitely male hand, the owner of the book had written:

It read like a directive to Jonathan himself. It also made him think. He had always judged himself to be a reasonably charitable person. But the more he thought the more he saw he was a meager and a grudging giver, justifying his chariness with the excuse that when he had more money he would give more. Now the entry in the datebook made him realize that his income and life circumstances were quite comfortable compared to those who were appealing for his help.

Rising from his chair again, he fetched the envelopes he had discarded earlier in the wastebasket. One by one he reread the letter each contained. The first was from a home for infirm children; the second from a school in a ghetto section of the city seeking funds for scholarships; the third was from a residence for senior citizens that had sustained a major fire and was hoping to rebuild. Within minutes, Jonathan wrote checks to all three charities, put stamps on the return envelopes, and placed them in the pocket of his overcoat to be mailed the next day.

What followed for him was a feeling of goodwill the likes of which Jonathan was unprepared to feel. Could it be, he wondered, that the simple act of charitable giving had produced such a sensation? Whatever the reason, Jonathan slept better that night than he had for many months.

The next morning was sunny and exceptionally mild, and Jonathan decided he would walk to work. At the mailbox on the corner of his street, he posted the envelopes with the enclosed checks he was sending, and as the flap of the mailbox slammed shut, he felt again the sense of pleasure and well-being he had known the night before.

When Jonathan arrived at Lost and Found he went directly to the shelves of unclaimed articles, took the datebook from his pocket, and slipped it in among some other items that began with *D* on a shelf. As he did he saw lying nearby a paisley scarf. Scarves belonged among the *S*'s, and he was about to take it to that section when he did something that for Jonathan was quite unusual. He picked up the scarf and instead spread it out across the datebook. Making certain that no portion of the book was visible, Jonathan proceeded to his desk.

The day was a particularly busy one for Lost and Found. Throughout it, Jonathan spent a good deal of his time assisting claimants who flocked to the department in an almost steady stream. Otherwise, he and Miss Brophy resumed a project they had started weeks before of listing alphabetically the unclaimed items on the shelves, today beginning with the letter *T*. (Among the *T*'s were a toupee, a set of false teeth, a torsade from a woman's hat, a child's toy trumpet, two ties, a tennis racket, and a tambourine.)

When the day ended, Jonathan exchanged good-nights with Felix and Miss Brophy, and began closing the department for the night. At last, he donned his overcoat, headed toward the doorway, turned off the lights, and was about to lock the door when a thought struck him.

Without turning on the lights again, he walked back to the shelves. He drew aside the paisley scarf, picked up the datebook, and held it in his hands. Even in the dim light from the hall the little *J* imprinted on the datebook's face shone with a golden sheen.

Jonathan debated with his conscience. What he was about to do, he knew, ran counter to procedure. But he decided there was nothing wrong in simply borrowing an unclaimed item overnight. If the owner of the datebook should appear tomorrow and make inquiries, it would be there waiting on the shelves—albeit underneath a paisley scarf.

Thus satisfied, he tucked the datebook in his jacket pocket and strode out the door.

Half an hour later, Jonathan hurried up the stairs to his apartment. Once inside, he took the datebook from his pocket and turned quickly to tomorrow's date—December 21. As he read the entry on the page, he felt his eyes begin to mist. He blinked, then read again.

Send gift to brother

said the page.

Jonathan folded shut the datebook. Then he laid his head back on the chair and closed his eyes.

His brother. As children they had been inseparable. Yet when both were in their twenties, a dispute had escalated into angry words. Each, finally, had vowed never to communicate again, and sadly, each had kept his vow. For years they had been totally estranged. His brother had moved to a distant city; Jonathan had not known where—or cared to know—until he'd read it in some legal papers following their mother's death.

His eyes still closed, he saw his brother in a montage of jumbled images—his brother's first tricycle, his brother on the school baseball team, his brother playing the harmonica . . .

Jonathan opened his eyes. He recalled especially how much his brother had loved to play a small harmonica he owned when they were boys. Over the years it had somehow come into Jonathan's possession.

Jonathan rose from his chair and went to the closet in his bedroom. Far back on the top shelf he found a box of family keepsakes, and removed the lid. Searching through the box, he found the object that he sought. The metallic surface of the harmonica was badly tarnished. But when Jonathan blew into it the sound was sweet and pure.

Before he went to bed that evening Jonathan located a small box with some tissue paper into which he cradled the harmonica. He was about to cover the box with gift paper when it occurred to him to add a note. In the note Jonathan extended Christmas greetings. He also spoke of the great bond that they had had as boys and regretted any hurt he might have caused. He also expressed the hope they could be real brothers once again. At last, he wrapped the note and the harmonica inside some mailing paper, and wrote his brother's name and address on the top.

That night while he lay in bed Jonathan made a decision. He was glad that he had taken home the book and read the entry in it for a second night. Tomorrow evening he would do the same. He wondered, in fact, if he should scan all the remaining pages and discover the additional surprises that awaited him. But that would spoil the anticipation he would have of reading each one singly the night before. No, he would not look ahead. He would take each entry in the datebook one by one, each day at a time.

But before sleep began to overcome him, Jonathan acknowledged he could hardly wait to know what new delight the entry he would read tomorrow night would bring.

Hang wreath

Hang wreath'?" Jonathan announced aloud. He stared down at the page. Early that morning, before heading to the store, he had gone to the post office and mailed the harmonica and note express delivery so that it would be in his brother's hands by Christmas. During the day that followed he had hardly been able to contain his eagerness to return home, read the datebook, and be told exactly what assignment was presented to him for the day ahead.

But now, looking at the entry for December 22, he was greatly disappointed. "Hang wreath" was all it said. To Jonathan, in fact, a wreath was the most clichéd of Christmas decorations. Wreaths turned brown and brittle almost instantly and began dropping needles within days. What's more, he was convinced that artificial greenery in late December, be it in the form of Christmas trees or wreaths or boughs, was an affront to nature's laws. Green might be appropriate for spring and summer, but not winter, when the dull and sullen tones of brown and gray held sway.

And just suppose he put a wreath on his apartment

door? What then? Who else but Jonathan himself would notice it? Certainly not Mrs. Gullett, who lived in the apartment opposite. He'd never seen her talk to anyone or anything, senile as she was, except the flower pattern on the wallpaper that lined their hall. Nor would that self-absorbed young couple at the far end of the hallway take the time to see it, less appreciate it, as they went about their daily lives.

Therefore, he made up his mind he would ignore the entry.

He ignored it after he awoke the morning of December 22.

He ignored it on his way to work, and throughout the hours that he spent in Lost and Found.

Although he retrieved the datebook from beneath the paisley scarf before he left that evening, he ignored it as he traveled home.

But as Jonathan walked toward his building from the bus stop at the corner of his street, he saw a sight that made him pause. Between two streetlights a thick rope had been strung. Against the rope were leaning half a dozen scrawny would-be Christmas trees. Hanging from the rope as well were several wreaths, none larger than a pie plate, but each one with a thin red bow attached. In the shadows of a nearby doorway, Jonathan observed as well, stood a boy in a threadbare coat. As Jonathan approached he realized the boy was the seller of the trees and wreaths. The lad, who could not have been older than thirteen, had taken shelter in a doorway to escape the wind. Still, now and then he peered out, looking up and down the street for customers.

A short time later, a small wreath with a red bow hung over the peephole in Jonathan's apartment door.

As Jonathan stepped back in the hall to see if it was straight, he heard a tiny voice speak.

"A wreath. How lovely," Mrs. Gullett said.

He turned to find her staring at the wreath. "Oh, bless you, you dear boy," Mrs. Gullett added, and bestowed on Jonathan a beatific smile.

"Look! A wreath!" said the young woman, as the couple from the far apartment stepped into the hall. "Let's get one for ourselves," she urged her husband, who was following behind.

"Good idea," said the young man. "Thanks for the idea," he told Jonathan as the couple started for the stairs. "And Merry Christmas, friend."

"Uh—Merry Christmas," answered Jonathan.

"Merry Christmas everybody," echoed Mrs. Gullett from her door.

Alone in the hall again, Jonathan looked once more at the little wreath. Then with one hand he patted the inside pocket of his jacket where the datebook lay.

Jonathan left the store before closing time the next evening so as to accomplish the directive in the datebook for that night.

December 23
Lighting of the tree

the datebook said.

It did not indicate which of the thousand trees around the city was to be lighted, nor did it tell him the location of that tree. For all he knew most major tree-lighting ceremonies had already taken place: local television news had shown so many it seemed every public evergreen had been subjected to a string or more of garish lights.

Then last night he had remembered the handwritten sign he'd seen. It had been posted on a wall beside a vacant lot in Jonathan's own neighborhood. The sign announced a tree lighting in the lot at six P.M., December 23.

The lot itself was bordered on three sides by long-abandoned tenements, their glassless windows staring down in blind despair. For years the lot had been a dumping ground for spent, unwanted waste, material and human both. But recently the homeless who had lived there amid the litter were relocated to a shelter, and the trash removed. Effort had been made to transform the lot into a tiny park: flower beds had been laid out, shrubs planted, several benches placed about. Last week in the lot also a slender pine tree had been set up, and its scrawny branches strung with lights.

This, Jonathan decided, was the tree-lighting ceremony he would attend.

Therefore, as the afternoon of December 23 wore on, Jonathan informed the other clerks he would be leaving early. Furthermore, he asked Miss Brophy if she would close the department for the night. To his surprise, Miss Brophy hesitated. She, too, had an engagement in the early evening, she told Jonathan. He acquiesced, and made the same request of Felix, who reluctantly agreed.

It was then minutes to six o'clock as Jonathan turned the corner of the street that held the vacant lot. Drawing nearer, he saw several dozen people in the lot, some standing, others seated on the benches. All were chatting amiably, although Jonathan guessed most of them had been strangers till tonight.

He stood at the edge of the assembled group. As he began to look around, he noticed an older gentleman move toward the Christmas tree and turn to face the crowd.

"My friends and neighbors," said the man. "Please join me in counting. . . . Ten—nine—eight— . . ."

The crowd took up the chant in unison. "Three—two—one."

Suddenly the tree burst into brilliant light. The crowd applauded.

"Now, the Christmas carols," said the gentleman. The next moment Jonathan felt a sheet of paper with the words of several carols being placed into his hand.

"Thank you," he began to murmur, when he looked up and saw the person who had handed him the paper—and who still stood before him—was Miss Brophy.

"You? Miss Brophy—do you live here? That is, do you live around here?"

"Yes sir." She was just as much embarrassed. "Yes, I do. Do you?"

"Yes. Yes. I do."

"Everyone now—'Joy to the World,'" called the gentleman beside the tree. He waved his arms conductor-fashion, and the group began to sing.

Miss Brophy had already moved on from where Jonathan stood, handing out the printed carols to the crowd. But as the people sang, and Jonathan sang with them, he observed her. Was this the woman he had worked with for four years? Her plain brown hair was covered by a white knitted hat. But in the bright glow from the lighted Christmas tree her eyes shone with a happiness and joy he had never seen before.

The carols ended, and as the crowd began dispersing, Jonathan searched for her within it. But she was nowhere to be seen. Still, as he walked home alone he also felt a certain joy he had not experienced in years. So strong did it become that he ducked into a lighted doorway, undid the topmost button of his overcoat, and reached into the inner pocket for the datebook. Withdrawing it, he flipped through the pages, stopping at tomorrow's date—December 24.

"Din—" he read beneath the date, until the cold blurred his sight. With a corner of his scarf he wiped his eyes. Then he peered down at the book again.

December 24
Dinner with her

Jonathan smiled to himself. It was as good as done. When he returned to his apartment, he would call that small French restaurant in the neighborhood where he had occasionally dined. Dinner for two tomorrow evening, he would tell them. That's right, just two people. Him and "her."

A traffic accident between a taxi and the bus on which Jonathan was traveling the next morning made him twenty minutes late for work, and by the time he hurried into Lost and Found Miss Brophy had arrived.

The delay was all the more upsetting to him since he

had hoped to be there well before her, and to have time to write her a discreet note concerning dinner for that night. But as he entered the department he saw she was already at the desk, cataloging items that had been turned in by the cleaning crews the night before.

Felix had also arrived before Jonathan, and was presently in conversation with a large gentleman at the claims counter in the front.

Jonathan was about to sit down at his own desk when he remembered that the datebook was still in the inside pocket of his suit. He stood again and walked to the aisle leading to the shelves of unclaimed articles. Stopping at the shelf that had the paisley scarf, he slipped the book underneath the scarf, and retraced his steps back to his desk.

Glancing briefly in Miss Brophy's direction as he sat down again, he pretended to be riffling through claim forms while he debated how best to approach her with his invitation for tonight.

A minute passed, then two—and it was only due to the distinct bass voice of the large man at the counter that Jonathan became aware of what was being said.

". . . Yes. It was a little datebook," the man was telling Felix. "Lost about a week ago, I think. . . ."

Jonathan's breath caught.

"I thought I might have left it in my office," the man added. "Or at home. . . ."

Jonathan rose and moved to the row of shelves nearest the counter, where he went through the motions of examining an unclaimed teddy bear.

"Then I remembered, I'd been shopping in the store that day," the man went on. "I thought I could've lost it here, and someone might have turned it in to Lost and Found. It's not all that important, really, since the year is almost done."

Felix snapped his gum and picked up the claim form that the man had already filled out.

Still clutching the teddy bear, Jonathan edged closer to the counter so he could read over the clerk's shoulder. On the form he saw the man's name: Joseph Jones.

"I'm sure there must be many like it," the man said to Felix. "Dark brown leather. The initial *J* stamped on the front in gold."

"I'll check the files," Felix told him. "But I don't remember seeing any datebook." He turned to Jonathan. "Do you?"

"No. No," Jonathan said at once. He shook his head vigorously.

"I saw a datebook."

Jonathan and Felix turned. Miss Brophy had now joined them. "Excuse me," she apologized, "but I overheard you mentioning a datebook. I saw one like it yesterday when I was looking through the *D*s. It was under a scarf. The scarf didn't belong there." She gave Jonathan a contrite look. "I meant to move it later, sir. But I forgot."

"I'll get it," Felix said. "Where is it?"

"Last aisle," she told him. "Under *D*. Third shelf from the top."

Felix headed toward the shelves, while the large man and Miss Brophy waited. Jonathan, on the other hand, clutched the teddy bear and stared across the counter at the man.

The man was obviously wealthy, self-assured. He made it seem as if the datebook's loss was probably no more than a minor inconvenience to him he could just as easily have done without. He had probably contributed to Christmas charities in any case. The man would have remembered to send a present to his brother, hang a wreath, and attend the lighting of a tree. The dinner invitation to "her" had certainly been issued days ago.

No, thought Jonathan, this Joseph Jones did not need entries in a datebook to engage himself in the events of life.

But Jonathan did.

"You found it!" The man brightened as Felix returned to the counter with the datebook in his hand.

The man took the datebook, opened it, and began flipping through the pages. After a short time his face took on a puzzled look.

"Amazing," the man said. "This datebook is exactly like the one I lost. Even the initial is the same. The J." He slapped the datebook on the counter. "But it isn't mine."

Felix shrugged. Miss Brophy gave the man a sympathetic smile. Jonathan began to breathe again.

The man thanked the three of them and walked out of Lost and Found. Felix carried the datebook in the direction of the shelves. Miss Brophy and Jonathan started back to their own desks.

Jonathan was about to sit once more when he discovered he was still clutching the teddy bear. He turned in the direction of the shelves and found Miss Brophy facing him, a tentative expression on her face.

"Mr. Jessup—" she said, hesitating. "May I ask you a question, sir?"

It was the opportunity he had been waiting for. "By all means," allowed Jonathan. "And I have a question for you when you're done."

"May I leave early, sir?"

He stared. "Tonight? You can't. I mean—"

"It's Christmas Eve. I promised Joe a special dinner."

"Who?"

"My Joe. I do a little something extra for him every Christmas Eve." She paused. "He's an old cat, and I love him very much."

Miss Brophy bowed her head. "I know I should have asked you sooner. But I'll make up the time somehow."

"Yes, you will," said Jonathan. "I mean, I hope you will tonight, Miss Brophy."

"Sir?"

"After Joe has had his dinner, that is . . ." he began.

By the time Jonathan returned to his apartment it was ten o'clock. Dinner with Miss Brophy had been charming. She had asked him, finally, to call her by her first name, Faith, and he in turn had relieved her of the formality of addressing him as "sir." He'd learned she lived alone (except for Joe the Cat), and that she, too, was seeking a fulfillment to her life. After dinner he had walked her back to her apartment. At the door they'd shaken hands and wished each other Merry Christmas.

Jonathan had then walked home.

Having had more wine than he intended, he fumbled with his door key just a bit. Once inside, it seemed to him that his apartment was extremely warm. He opened a window, then removed his overcoat and went to hang it in the closet. As he did, he saw his own face in the mirror on the inside of the closet door. It was flushed. The wine again, he thought.

Or was it more than that? Was it the evening with Miss Brophy that had brought such color to his face? In no way had the time they spent incited stirrings of romance. What Jonathan had felt this evening in Miss—in Faith's—company was almost better. Sitting in the restaurant opposite her he had realized that she was someone who could be a friend—someone with whom he could share his honest thoughts and feelings, and who in turn could trust in sharing hers with him. If such a friendship led to romance then so be it. Now the future held a host of possibilities for Jonathan, and he would value every one.

The future. He repeated the two words to himself. Less than a week ago he had looked upon it as a void. Then inexplicably the datebook had appeared in Lost and Found, and it had changed his life.

The *datebook*, Jonathan remembered. He must read the entry for tomorrow, for December 25. Of all the pleasures and surprises that the little book had given him, the one for Christmas had to be the best of all!

With fingers trembling, Jonathan thrust a hand into the inside pocket of his suit. He touched his eyeglass case and drew it out. He reached again. The datebook was not there.

Hurriedly, he checked the outer pockets of his jacket. Nothing.

Neither was the datebook in his trousers.

Suddenly Jonathan thought back to the time he had been closing up the Lost and Found department for the evening. He'd been looking forward with such pleasure to the dinner with Faith Brophy that the datebook had completely slipped his mind.

Jonathan knew what he had to do. He would race immediately to the store, make some excuse to the guards to let him in, then go to Lost and Found and get the book from where Felix had returned it to the shelves.

He went directly to his closet, flung aside the door, and grabbed his overcoat. Plunging one arm, then the other, into the sleeves, he again glimpsed his reflection in the mirror of the door.

"I need the book!" he shouted to the image of himself he saw.

He stopped, and stared into the mirror, moving his face closer slowly till it filled the glass. What he saw now made Jonathan ashamed. The person staring back at him was fearful, desperate. This was not the confident, the hopeful, man he was becoming with the datebook's help. The daily entries in the book had been the catalyst for his reentry into life. But that was all they could or should be.

Starting with tomorrow—and for the remainder of his life—the way he chose to fill his days was up to Jonathan alone.

Arising early Christmas morning, and dressed in his best suit, Jonathan left his apartment and ventured out among the city streets. The weather was as fine and clear as any Christmas Day he could recall, and he walked with a brisk step. The boy in the neighborhood, from whom he'd bought the wreath, today was only selling holly sprigs out of his pockets. Jonathan purchased the largest and most colorful, and pinned it to his coat lapel.

The city had never seemed more festive or more friendly than it did to him that day. Everywhere he walked passersby smiled and bestowed greetings of the season, which he always hastened to return. He lunched at a restaurant where the waitress asked his name and gave him extra giblet gravy as a special Christmas treat.

In the afternoon he ambled to the skating rink within the park, where he watched the skaters, many in bright-colored outfits, gliding everywhere about the ice. Jonathan rented a pair of ice skates for himself, and despite a spill that landed him among some squealing teenage girls, he skated for an hour with the crowd.

As the day began to wane and darkness came, a chill breeze stirred the air. But Jonathan was unaware of it, warmed as he was by the spirit of the holiday he'd spent.

When he returned to his apartment it was much later than he thought. Opening the door, he heard his telephone begin to ring. The call was from his brother. For an hour the two spoke, sharing moments of the lives that each had led in recent years. Before the phone call ended, his brother played a tune on the harmonica.

In the week that followed, Jonathan's life was fuller and more rich than it had ever been. He attended plays and concerts, visited museums, and dined again with Faith, who later invited him into her apartment briefly to meet Joe the Cat.

Indeed, Jonathan became so busy he could barely keep in mind all the activities he'd planned. Several times, he was tempted to take the little datebook from the shelves of Lost and Found (it now sat fully visible among the *D*'s) and use it for himself; or simply out of curiosity, read what entries had been written in it between Christmas and the last day of the year. But he did not.

Instead, late in the afternoon of December 31, Jonathan went to the Stationery section of the store. There he purchased a new datebook for the year ahead that would begin that night. Its covers were of dark brown leather. On the front of it, in gold, he requested that they stamp the letter *J*.

SNOW CHILDREN

*T*he Year Without Snow it had been called. Since January last, and throughout the winter months, there had been sleet enough to stifle traffic on the city streets. But at no time was there a snowfall of any measurable depth. Now it was December, the twelfth month of that year, and still only a few capricious snowflakes had been seen floating from the sky. Fewer still had touched earth, all to disappear as quickly as they came. Adults, of course, did not complain. For them snow was an annoyance, an interruption in their workaday routine. It was the children, on the other hand, who suffered most. Sleds received a year ago sat idle and unslid upon; no snowmen had been fashioned, nor a single snowball thrown.

Of all the children, none seemed more acutely disappointed than the twins; a boy and a girl. For their seventh birthday in October, their parents had given them red knitted hats with a design of white snowflakes circling the base. Matching also were their dark blue coats and yellow boots, their red mittens and red scarves.

The boy's name was Schuyler, although everybody called him Skipper. His sister was Samantha. Samantha was addressed by no other name than that, and anyone who dared to call her Sam was greeted with a frosty stare. Both children had blond hair, large blue eyes, and full round faces that gave them an endearingly cherubic look. Their only visible distinction, other than Samantha's curls, was that Skipper's nose ran constantly from the beginning of October to the end of March.

But the twins were different in several other ways as well. Samantha, who had been born twenty minutes earlier, was the more serious and realistic of the two. Contrarily, her brother seemed at times to live with pleasure in a world of his own imaginings. If he found a penny lying in the street, it was transformed in his retelling into a rare gold coin. Skipper's parents had tried often to correct this tendency toward fabrication. As adults they knew with sober certainty that rare gold coins did not simply lie about in public waiting to be found.

So it was with some reluctance that the twins' mother agreed to take them to the Toy section of the store. For if there was any corner of the great establishment where fantasy and make-believe were most enthusiastically encouraged, it was Toys. Nonetheless, she had decided Toys would be their final stop after all her other Christmas shopping had been done. The twins' father, who happened to work in the same neighborhood, had planned to join them, and afterward accompany his family home.

The mother paused as she approached the aisle that led into Toys. Then she pointed to a pair of giant red-and-white-striped candy canes that framed the entrance.

"Wait here while I call your father's office," she said to the children. "Stand next to those candy canes. And don't get mixed up with the crowds."

Dutifully, Samantha walked directly to the nearest cane and wrapped an arm around it. Skipper went and stood beside the other.

"Put your arm around it, Skipper," said the mother.

Skipper made a face, but put one arm around the candy cane.

"Good." The mother smiled at them both. "Now will you promise you won't move from there till I get back?"

"I promise," said Samantha.

"Uh huh," Skipper said.

The mother smiled for a second time, and headed off across the floor. Skipper and Samantha watched her go. Then Skipper let his eyes travel up along the candy cane beside him. Like the one to which his sister clung, it was a foot wide and reached almost to the high ceiling before curving in a graceful arc.

"I wish I had a candy cane this big," he said.

"They don't make candy canes as big as this," Samantha said with certainty. "These aren't real. They're just big wooden poles painted red and white."

The boy shrugged. Instead of telling her how nice they'd be if they *were* real, he studied the displays of toys that awaited them. Nearby was a row of shiny racing bicycles with more attachments on the handlebars than he could count. Although Skipper had only recently begun to learn to ride a bicycle, he considered telling all his friends at school that on his visit to the Toy section of the store today, a clerk had placed him on a sleek new ten-speed model and encouraged him to race it up and down the aisle, which Skipper had gone on to do, to the delight and wonder of the crowd.

His arm began to ache from clutching at the candy cane. So he let go of it, and stepped into the aisle, while he moved his shoulders back and forth.

Suddenly, he felt the collar of his coat seized from behind; the next instant, he was moving backward at such speed that his feet hardly had a chance to touch the floor.

"Don't try to hide from me!" he heard a woman's voice say.

He tried digging in his heels, but kept skidding in reverse so swiftly that he had no time to catch his breath or call for help. It occurred to Skipper he was being kidnapped, and he swung his arms to try to free himself without success.

Then, just as suddenly, the hand that grasped the collar of his coat let go of it, and Skipper was immediately spun around. Breathless, he discovered he was face-to-face with a behemoth of a woman in a quilted orange coat.

"*Bad boy*, Christopher!" The woman scolded, fingers splayed. "You sneak away from me like that again and you're—" The woman stared, her mouth fell open, and a little gasp ensued. "Oh, dear. You're not my Christopher . . . !"

The woman crossed her hands against her chest,

repeated "Oh, dear" twice, then turned and fled, her plaintive cries of "Christopher?" resounding through the store.

Skipper stood for several moments, too bewildered to do anything. He looked around. The large woman in the orange coat was nowhere to be seen. But neither were the giant candy canes. Still, from the display of model airplanes beside him, he decided he was somewhere well within the Toy section. Skipper also knew that he was lost.

He mustn't cry, he told himself. He was seven years, plus several months, of age, and he would act it. Crying was what babies did. Then he remembered what his mother had told both the twins to do if they became separated from her on occasions such as this. Seek out a salesclerk, she had instructed them; repeat your first and last names in a good clear voice, and announce that you are lost.

Unfortunately, though the aisle where he stood was filled with people, not a single person seemed to be a clerk. So cautiously, and having no idea where the aisle led, Skipper began walking in the direction that he thought the candy canes might be. When the aisle became too crowded for him to proceed, he turned into a second aisle, where a rolling stock cart full of merchandise soon blocked his way.

He turned around and headed into a third aisle.

Then another . . .

And another—when he saw the table.

It was small and wooden, and the legs appeared to have been recently repaired. The surface of the table was at the level of the boy's eyes, and Skipper somehow felt drawn to examine it. Placed randomly about it were several dozen round glass globes, each nesting on a painted base. Skipper noticed that each globe also held a different Christmas scene inside. The one nearest him had a figure of a Santa Claus. One of Santa's hands was waving in a jolly greeting, while on his shoulder he held a toy-laden sack.

Skipper picked up the globe, studied it, then shook it hard. As he did, tiny specks of white flew up around the Santa Claus. The harder Skipper shook the globe, the more the snowflakes swirled in a miniature blizzard that raged 'round and 'round inside the globe.

The boy set the globe down on the table and watched the snowflakes gradually begin to settle toward the base. As they did, the Santa Claus was visible once more, the sack still on his shoulder, his hand still lifted in an eternal gesture of salute.

Skipper pressed closer to the table and inspected the other snow globes. One contained a tiny model of a forest cabin. Beside the cabin was a pine tree with a star on top. Inside another globe there was a group of animals—a deer, a fox, a rabbit, and a bear. A third globe featured a quartet of Christmas carolers with lanterns all aglow. The mouth of each caroler was open wide, as if in song. Skipper picked up the globe and put it to his ear. No carols sounded though the glass. He gave the globe a momentary shake as well, and watched as the snow specks rose up to obliterate the singers in a cloud of white.

Then, momentarily, a flash of light reflected off a globe he had not noticed earlier. It sat well behind the others at the far side of the table, and it was smaller than the rest.

Standing on his toes, Skipper stretched his arms as

long as he could reach across the table, and put his hands around the globe. He lifted it and brought it toward him, cradling it gently in his palms. Inside the snow globe were two figures—a boy and a girl. They appeared to Skipper also to be twins. What's more, they were dressed in red hats, scarves, and mittens, with blue coats and yellow boots.

Skipper put the globe against one eye and squinted through the glass to get a better look. To his surprise, the eyes of the children in the globe seemed to be staring back at him. Their arms hung at their sides. Their mouths were tightly closed. And in place of the smiling faces Skipper had expected, theirs seemed filled with fear.

The boy stepped back from the table and held the globe out at arm's length. He shook it. As he did, the white flakes spiraled up, surrounding the two little figures, obscuring them from view.

Drawing the globe close again, he waited for the snow to settle. As it began to do so, Skipper stared in disbelief. The arms of the two tiny figures now reached out in his direction, and their mouths were open in a mute appeal for his help.

A hand touched Skipper's shoulder.

Skipper jumped. He swung around—and found Samantha facing him.

"I've been looking for you everywhere," his sister told him. "I chased after that woman when she grabbed you. And got lost."

"I guess we're both lost now," the boy said. "We ought to try to find the candy canes."

But Samantha didn't answer. Instead, she had been looking at the snow globe in her brother's hand.

"What's that?" the girl asked him.

Skipper hesitated. "You know—it's a glass with stuff that looks like snow inside it."

"Can I see it?"

"There's others on the table."

"I want to see the one you've got."

The boy hesitated. Then he offered it reluctantly.

His sister took it from his hands and looked at it. "Did you see this?" she said. "It's got two children in it just like us." She began to shake it.

"Don't!"

Samantha stopped. But she was visibly annoyed. "You're supposed to shake it for the snow to fly around."

"Just don't."

"I will unless you tell me why."

"Because . . ." He knew what her response would be, but said it anyway. "Because the children in the globe . . . are real."

What surprised him was that she said nothing. She glanced briefly at the globe, then eyed him skeptically. "They're made of plastic. How can they be real?"

"Look at their faces," Skipper urged her. "They're afraid."

"Of what?"

"I don't know. But *look*."

Samantha raised the globe again and pressed it close against her face. She breathed on the glass, wiped the condensation with her hand, and stared at it again.

"When I picked up the globe," the boy said, "their arms were down. But then I shook it. And after the snow cleared their arms were up. Like this." He demonstrated with his own. "I even think they were trying to call out to me."

"Skipper!"

"I'm not making it up."

"You are."

"I'm *not*."

"There's only one way to find out," Samantha said.

Before Skipper could react, Samantha gave the globe a sudden shake. Immediately snow obscured everything inside the glass. Watching it intently now, she placed the snow globe on the table. Very gradually, the topmost portion began to clear. As the tiny flakes continued falling, Samantha's face took on an aspect of incredulous surprise.

"Look there!" She thrust a finger at the globe.

Inside it, the figures of the children stood against the glass, their hands upraised, their mouths open as if both were calling desperately for help.

"How did they get in there?" she asked.

"I don't know. Maybe they're like genies put in bottles."

"We've got to tell someone. A clerk or somebody. They'll know what to do."

The boy thought. "I hope so," Skipper said. But he did not look thoroughly convinced.

Even so, the twins began to make their way together through the aisles of the Toy section of the store. Skipper walked ahead. Samantha followed several steps behind, her red scarf wrapped around the globe, which was clutched tightly in her hands. The giant candy canes were nowhere to be seen. But finding them was not their goal now; what mattered only was to help the tiny figures trapped inside the globe.

Past puzzles, puppet theaters, and paint sets the twins walked. Past model trains and music boxes; roller skates and rocket ships; dolls and drums and dinosaurs; huge stuffed bears and building blocks; and wind-up clowns that leaped and cartwheeled on a tabletop as the twins watched.

Many of the aisles that they ventured down were jammed with people—clerks attending customers; parents with their children; even older men and women, who like children were delighting in the wonderland of fun and fantasy created there. But at no time did Skipper or Samantha see anyone they believed could be entrusted with the secret of the globe.

Time passed, and after walking for they didn't know how long, they found themselves within a small enclosure where, to their surprise, the twins saw no one. The hanging birchwood sign above their heads said CAMPERS' CORNER. The space had been arranged so as to resemble a clearing in the woods. In the center of it was a khaki-colored pup tent. Around it, several imitation tree stumps added to the sylvan scene. Beside the tent, small logs were piled up into a realistic-looking campfire that smoldered red within.

Skipper and Samantha sat down on tree stumps facing each other. Carefully, the girl drew her scarf to one side and together the twins looked down at the globe. The figures were once more standing at the center of it.

But now their hands were to their eyes.

"I think they're crying," Samantha said, peering at the globe.

The boy was aware that his own eyes had begun to fill with tears.

"We've got to get them out," she went on. "Maybe we can take the globe apart."

"What? Here?"

Samantha glanced around. Her eyes fell on the tent. "In there." She pointed. "We'll open it inside the tent."

"But—"

"Go on. Lift the flap."

Skipper took a deep breath and knelt down before the tent. He pulled aside the flap and crawled inside. His sister followed, carrying the globe. Once in, she drew the tent flap back in place, so that the only light came throught the coarse fabric of the tent itself. In the dimness she held out the globe in his direction.

"Here. You do it."

"Why me?"

"Because boys are supposed to be better with their hands."

Skipper looked at his own hands, then at hers. Still, he took the globe. With his right hand he grasped the base. He spread the fingers of his left hand across the top. Very slowly he began to twist. He grunted once. It did not help.

Frowning, Skipper lifted his fingers from the globe and flexed them. Next he wiped them on his coat. He blew on them. Finally, he placed them on the globe again, and twisted harder. He shut his eyes once more, and turned his head away.

Still nothing.

A long deep breath. Another twist. A grunt. A third twist. "It's no use," Skipper finally admitted.

"Wait here," Samantha said.

She turned from him and crept out of the tent. Within a few minutes, she returned carrying a small plastic case with a handle that looked like a child's lunchbox.

"What's that?" Skipper asked.

"A Junior Builder kit." She held it up. "I saw it on a table that we passed two aisles back."

Samantha knelt down beside him, placed the kit in front of them, and snapped open the lid. Inside it were a variety of tools—a hammer, a brace and bit, a screwdriver, a handsaw, and a drill—all of them reduced in size to fit a child's hand.

She took the hammer from the case and offered it.

"Use this," she instructed Skipper.

"It's a hammer."

"Of course it's a hammer. Use it to break the glass."

"But it'll hurt the children."

"Not if you tap lightly." She swung the hammer up and down, demonstrating for his benefit. "Crack the glass, that's all. We'll pour the water off, or whatever's inside, and help the children to climb out."

"I'm not so sure," the boy said. "I'm scared."

"*Skipper.*"

Reluctantly he took the hammer from her hand.

"Okay," he said. "Here goes."

He put the snow globe between his knees. He pulled one of his wool mittens from a pocket of his coat and placed it over the top of the globe.

"Why did you do that?" Samantha asked.

"In case a piece of glass falls out, I won't get cut."
He didn't mention it would also prevent his seeing the
two little figures as he struck the blows.

"All right," Samantha said. "Now hit it."

Skipper held the hammer just above the globe and
gave the mitten several gentle taps.

"Harder."

Skipper hesitated.

"Go ahead."

He placed the hammer somewhat higher.

"Go on. *Hit* it."

Skipper swung the hammer. As it hit, he heard what
sounded like a crack.

"*Again!*"

Again the hammer struck. There was a second
cracking sound far louder than the first: another crack
and then another and another. Skipper pulled the mitten
from the globe and stared. A million tiny lines were
radiating downward everywhere around the glass.

"Samantha! Look!" The boy gasped.

Suddenly there was a brilliant light, and an explo-
sion as if from the bursting of a million stars. . . . Then
darkness. Silence. Space—impenetrable, absolute, and
infinite, through which the twins fell spinning . . . spinning . . . spinning—slow and peaceful and serene as
flakes of snow. . . .

S tep back!"—"Please stand away."—"There's been an
accident."—"Is anybody here a doctor?"—"Stand
back!"

Voices, words mixing in a jumble came to them.

The twins opened their eyes. The tent was gone. Above them they saw lights and unfamiliar anxious faces. Hands reached down, more voices were heard.

"What happened?"

"Someone saw them carrying a snow globe."

"Thing must've exploded. Probably pressurized."

"Amazing they weren't cut by glass."

"What're all those little white specks?"

"Snowflakes."

"What do you mean snowflakes?"

"From inside the globe."

The crowd parted and a man appeared. He knelt down. "I'm a doctor," he said softly to the twins. "Can you hear me?"

Skipper and Samantha turned their heads toward him. They nodded.

While several clerks and an officer from store security encouraged the onlookers to disperse, the doctor made a quick examination of them both. "Can you sit up?" he asked when he was done.

Again, the children nodded.

Carefully, the doctor raised them, first the boy, then the girl, into a sitting position on the floor. Blinking, the children gazed around. The tent lay crumpled to one side. The logs of the campfire were scattered, and tiny white flecks covered everything. Nearby, the twins also saw Skipper's mitten and the hammer from the Junior Builder kit.

The next moment two arms eagerly embraced them. "Oh, my children," cried the mother.

"Just a little shock," the doctor told her. He explained what probably had caused the accident. He added that in his judgment neither child had been hurt.

Their mother hugged the twins a second time, and they saw tears of joy and relief in her eyes. "What happened?" she asked them.

"There were two little children in the globe," said Skipper. "We were trying to get them out."

"That's why we broke the globe," Samantha said.

The doctor interceded. He spoke smoothly to the mother. "The experience has startled them. They're still disoriented; they're imagining things from the brief time they were unconscious. It will pass."

After some minutes in which the security man wrote down details of the incident, and the crowd was finally persuaded to move on, the mother, doctor, and a salesclerk helped Skipper and Samantha to their feet.

The doctor reassured their mother that he thought the children would be fine. He bid them all good-bye, gave each twin a friendly pat, and headed off.

Holding tightly to their mother's hands, and guided by the salesclerk, the twins slowly walked back through the Toy section to the giant candy canes. They found their father waiting for his family there. When he learned of the twins' misadventure, he too hugged the children. Neither one of them was hurt, he said, and that's what mattered most.

He also had a wonderful idea. Since the twins had obviously loved the snow globe best of the toys they had seen, he suggested that as soon as both had gotten over what had happened, the family would revisit the department store, return to Toys, and let the children choose another snow globe to replace the one that broke.

Skipper and Samantha glanced at one another. Then they shook their heads.

Presently, clutching the hands of both their parents, the twins left the store. Members of the store's cleaning staff attended to the disarray in Campers' Corner, sweeping up the bits of broken glass and sticky liquid from inside the globe. Several clerks and a store decorator reset the campfire, rearranged the tree stumps, and put up the fallen tent. In the Toy section itself, shoppers once again moved freely through the aisles admiring the displays.

As for the doctor, he had remained in the store after the incident to complete some Christmas shopping of his own. It was only as he was preparing to depart that a curious event occurred. He was among a large group that was exiting the main doors of the store. Since most customers bore shopping bag or packages, everyone moved slowly. Others slowed the crowd's momentum by stopping to adjust their hats and scarves and coat collars before stepping out into the cold gray afternoon.

Then in an instant, as the crush of people momentarily parted, the doctor was startled by the sight he saw. Among the throngs were two young children. He could not see their faces, but from the back they looked exactly like the pair he had attended to in Toys—blue coats with yellow boots, red scarves, and matching red wool hats. Tiny specks of white were also visible against their coats and hats.

In fact, the doctor finally assumed these *were* the children he had aided earlier that day. What surprised him was that they seemed to be alone, and not in the company of an adult. But remembering their mother's great concern for them, he was sure she must be some-where in the crowd.

Now the doctor himself moved through the doors and stepped out onto the sidewalk bordering the store. As he did he was aware of something on his face. He looked up at the sky and realized it had begun to snow. He thought then of the snow globe that the twins had spoken of. The doctor, too, had loved snow globes as a child. He recalled with wistful memory the many times he'd held one in his hands and shaken it. Once he had even owned a globe within which were the figures of a boy and a girl. Looking back across the years, it sad-dened him a bit to think how often he had gazed in rapt attention as the snowflakes swirled up around them—and how much in his childish imagination he had wanted to believe that they were real.

THE
BOOKWORM

*Y*ou can't tell a book by its cover." Oliver
invariably used that phrase whenever he re-
told the story, even months after it occurred. Since he
had been employed by the Books department of the
store for many years, and was its senior salesman, the
words seemed all the more appropriate.

It was the last morning of November when he remembered noticing the man for the first time. Because
Oliver was short of stature he kept a little platform near
the register, so that he could stand on it from time to
time and have an overview of his domain. He had been
standing on the platform for perhaps a minute, peering
through his rimless glasses, when his attention was
drawn to a gentleman standing at a table that contained
Christmas books. Why his focus fell on this one man
among the many shoppers in his section, Oliver had no

idea. There was nothing in the man's appearance that distinguished him in any way. He was probably in his fifties; with curly gray hair, and a face unremarkable in all respects, he seemed the most anonymous of men.

As Oliver continued watching, the man left the Christmas books and moved on to another table, scanning the variety of titles on display. A browser, not a purchaser, thought Oliver, and dismissed the fellow from his mind.

He was surprised, therefore, to see the man again that afternoon. This time, as Oliver stood on his platform, he observed the man facing a set of shelves not far from the register. The shelf he was studying contained a set of classic works by English authors—Hardy, Trollope, Wilde, and the like. The man's right hand was lifted to the shelf, the index finger lightly touching each title as it went. At last the finger paused, the other fingers rose to join it, and the hand withdrew a volume from the shelf.

The man opened the book and slowly began thumbing through the pages. The books were leatherbound, the titles and the authors stamped in gold on the spine; the edges of the pages were gilt as well. There was also a small ribbon of red silk attached to the top so as to serve as a bookmark. The man ceased his thumbing, opened the book fully, and gazed down. Finally, he placed the red silk ribbon between the open pages, closed the book, and returned it once more to the shelf. Smiling to himself, the man turned and eased on toward the crowds that filled the floor.

Curious at what he'd witnessed, Oliver stepped down from his platform and walked to the same bookshelf where the man had stood. He found the book in which the man had repositioned the ribbon. The volume was a collection of the works of Charles Dickens, and mindful of the approaching holiday, Oliver wondered if the fellow had sought out Dickens's *A Christmas Carol*, which was always popular about this time of year.

Instead, Oliver discovered that the ribbon had been placed at the beginning of a set of very minor stories by the English master. Oliver read several paragraphs, none of which had anything to do with Christmas. Closing the book, Oliver admitted to himself that he was puzzled.

His puzzlement was increased further when he recalled the incident for the other members of the Books department later in the day. The sales staff included Martha, a woman who like Oliver was in her fifties, and who treated customers with the effusion of a chatty nanny; Beatrice, a tall thin woman close to forty who had once worked in a rare books library and wore her hair tied back in a rigid little bun; and Roger, a scholarly young man who was striving for a doctorate in lexicography.

After Oliver had finished telling of the man, Martha remembered she had seen the very same person earlier that week. She had been tidying a table of best-sellers, Martha mentioned, when he had appeared opposite her, his nose buried in a book. Martha recognized the title.

"It's really quite good," Martha had said brightly to the gentleman. "I finished it last night."

The man looked up without expression and regarded her.

"It received wonderful reviews," she'd added. "But perhaps you read them?"

The man had stared at her, then shook his head, set down the book, and moved away.

"I bet he was the same one I saw," Beatrice then said. She'd been approaching the small corner of the section that sold books of poetry when she noticed a man seated on a step stool of the sort clerks used for reaching volumes on high shelves. A book of poems had sat lovingly in his hands. On his face had been a look of such beatification as she had ever seen.

"Who was he?" each one of the clerks asked the others.

Opinions were expressed. He was not their average customer, they agreed, that much was sure. He was not a customer at all, the truth was, since he hadn't bought a single book. But Oliver admitted that the gentleman was not the idle browser he had first considered him. Mostly, browsers flitted from one book to another. To the contrary, the stranger lingered over every one.

"In fact, he seems to burrow into every book he touches," Oliver suggested.

"Like *Larvaeus bibliocacous*," Roger added wryly.

"What on earth is that?" asked Beatrice.

"The bookworm," Roger said.

Throughout the week that followed, the unassuming gentleman (whom the four clerks now referred to as the Bookworm), continued to return to their department, sometimes twice a day. Roger told the others he had watched the man engrossed for half an hour in a classic volume about marriage rites in the Samoan Islands. Beatrice reported she had seen him fingering a book of verses that had been translated into English from the Greek. Martha burbled over with the news one evening that she'd stood behind him as he'd examined dozens of biographies that ranged from famous popes of history to purple profiles of aging movie queens.

Speculation as to the man's profession naturally ensued. Oliver believed that he was probably a scholar, although why he didn't use a library instead remained unclear. He was a literary critic, someone ventured. He was the editor of an esoteric small review, another said. And still more theories were advanced—the man was possibly a linguist, a philologist, an etymologist. They all agreed, however, that one fact was indisputable. The awe and reverence with which he studied every volume marked him as a total devotee of that most precious of commodities—the written word.

It was the morning of the second week when Oliver informed the others that their curiosity and idle speculation had gone on long enough. When the Bookworm reappeared in Books that day, as certainly he would, Oliver intended to confront him and demand—request, that is—an explanation for his frequent presence in their midst.

Less than an hour after that, the opportunity arose. Informed by Roger that the Bookworm had been spotted near the travel books, Oliver walked directly to that section. The man stood with his back to him, flipping through the pages of a book on Bali he had taken from the shelves.

"Excuse me," said Oliver. He cleared his throat. "Sir?"

The man did not appear to hear him. Oliver edged over to the side. "Sir . . ." said Oliver again.

The man turned. He blinked several times. "Yes?"

"If I may say so, sir . . ." Oliver began to hesitate. Direct confrontation wouldn't do. "That is," he went on, "the others of the sales staff and I have seen you here on numerous occasions. And we wondered if— If you've been searching for a book you couldn't find."

The man looked hard at Oliver. It made him exceedingly uncomfortable.

"No," the man said, finally. He shook his head and quickly put the book back on the shelf. "I'm sorry if my visits bother you."

"Oh, not at all," Oliver assured him. Looking at him now, Oliver felt awkward. Acute embarrassment showed on the man's face.

"It's just . . . We thought . . . If we can be of help to you in any way—please do not hesitate to ask."

The man considered this. "Thank you," he told Oliver. Then he turned and left the Books department at an unnaturally swift pace.

Perhaps because of his exchange with Oliver, the man was nowhere to been seen in Books for several days. When he finally returned he remained at the farthest corner of the section, glancing nervously around him as he scanned the shelves.

The department was particularly busy that day. The four clerks had acknowledged the man's presence, and then put him from their minds. So when Beatrice noticed him moving toward the shelves on which the books of poetry were kept, she gave it no particular significance at first. But when she saw the man take down a slim volume which she knew to be the works of the French poet Baudelaire, it struck her like a thunderbolt.

"Of course!" she told herself. She should have recognized him instantly. The face. The gestures. Everything. She went on staring in the man's direction.

Yes. It had to be. It *was*.

The unknown man, the stranger Roger had so cavalierly called the Bookworm, was himself a noted poet. Beatrice was sure. In college she had read everything he'd written; indeed, she had devoured the details of his life with an intensity that bordered on idolatry. Yet as celebrated as he was in literary circles, he was also known for his reclusiveness. He had never married, lived a hermetical existence in his woodland atelier, and had sworn the few acquaintances he had to total public silence on his personal behalf. He was the subject of no recent photographs; Beatrice could recall only one of him as a young man in his twenties, when he and a beautiful Italian poetess of whom he was enamored had been discovered in a water taxi on the Grand Canal.

Looking at him here today, even from a distance of three aisles, Beatrice was more convinced than ever it was he. In her mind's eye, she compared the features of this man with that photograph of long ago. The hair was gray now, but still curly; the face that had been so smooth and pale was now considerably lined.

Then Beatrice observed the hands. They were a poet's hands, undoubtedly. She remembered from the photo how exceptionally long and thin the fingers were. The hands that held the Baudelaire today could be identical to those of years ago; the hands of a great poet cradling the volume of another whose own words cried out with the same exquisite despair.

"What's going on?" a voice asked. Beatrice turned to discover Roger standing at her side.

"He's *here*," she whispered. "Look. The shelves of poetry."

"Of course he's here," said Roger. "He's been here for two weeks."

Beatrice pulled Roger close to her and spoke the great man's name. "It is. I know," she said.

Roger blinked, and pressed his lips, then looked over at the man. He caught his breath. "Amazing. But I think you're right. We have to tell Oliver and Martha."

Seeking out the other clerks at once, they announced their startling discovery. Martha, although agreeing there was a strong resemblance to the much-honored poet, couldn't understand why he should be visiting their little section of the store day after day.

"Perhaps he comes here," answered Oliver, "to draw inspiration from the works of other poets, other writers. I admit it seems preposterous—a literary giant such as he is, and a recluse, deciding to appear in public in a department store at Christmastime. Still, the man is a creative genius who has always had disdain for the conventional. His very life has been a celebration of the unexpected."

Oliver looked back in the direction of the Bookworm. By now he had moved onto another section and was studying a shelf of mysteries.

"Appropriate," mused Oliver. "Our man of mystery is known at last."

When he reappeared at three o'clock that afternoon the clerks were ready. Roger saw him first. He signaled with a hand to Beatrice, who sought out Martha, who, in turn, waved Oliver down from his platform near the register.

"He's heading toward the children's books," Oliver told the others as he joined them.

"Of course he is," sighed Martha. "Only a child and a poet possess the innocence and clarity of vision to see life as it truly is."

Together in a little band, the four marched to where the man was standing, studying a picture book of Mother Goose. It had been agreed that Oliver, as senior salesman, would speak for all of them.

"Ah-hem," said Oliver as he approached the man.

The man looked up. He regarded Oliver with a vague hint of recognition, but said nothing.

"Sir—permit me to express the honor you've bestowed upon us by your visit to our section of the store."

The man glanced from one person to the next. Roger nodded. Martha opened her mouth. Beatrice gave him a quick smile and immediately dropped her eyes.

Now from behind his back Oliver withdrew a slender volume, which he proceeded to display for the man's benefit. "Sir—I'm sure you recognize this as your most recent collection of poetic works. A splendid book, if I may add. We—the other members of the staff and I—would be most grateful if you'd autograph it for us."

Oliver opened the volume to the title page and thrust it in the direction of the man.

The man stared down at the small book. "I can't do that," he said.

Beatrice noticed his discomfort. "Sir," she said, "could you at least read the opening lines of the poem that I find most beautiful. Please?"

She took the book from Oliver, turned quickly to the page, and held out the open book before the man.

The man's eyes darted back and forth across the pages. He looked at Beatrice at last, and shook his head.

"Perhaps a single line then," Beatrice beseeched him.

"No."

"To hear your voice, just—"

"I can't," he interrupted her. "I can't do that. . . ." His eyes now took on an anguished quality. "I can't— read very much at all," he said.

The four were silent. Roger's forehead furled. Martha bit her lip. Beatrice seemed not to comprehend. Oliver withdrew the book of poetry from Beatrice's still outstretched hands.

"Are we to understand, sir, that you are not the author of this volume?" Oliver asked.

"No."

Oliver frowned, as if he had been personally duped. "Then can you explain to us why you have been coming here day after day? From what we have observed, you seemed determined to read every book in stock."

"I haven't read them," the man said.

"Be that as it may—"

"I can't."

"Can't what?"

"Can't read. I'm trying to learn," the man said. "I have to, you see. For Christmas."

Slowly, very slowly, Oliver closed the book of poetry.

"Martha . . . Roger . . . Beatrice . . ." he told the others. "Please attend to customers. The gentleman and I—will have some private words. . . ."

Those who had heard only the beginning of this story guessed at a variety of reasons for the man's behavior when confronted by the four. The first, and least charitable, was that he was a notorious shoplifter, and that his repeated visits were part of a sophisticated ruse to steal books when the Christmas shopping crowds were at their peak. The second theory was that the man was excessively withdrawn and shy, and that those feelings were compounded when the four mistook him for the famous poet. Others speculated that he was indeed the famous poet, but because he was so determinedly reclusive, he not only lied about his true identity, he also mocked the world by denying he could even read.

The truth, however, was exactly as the man had stated it. He could not read. He repeated it again to Oliver when they'd sat down together on step stools in a quiet corner of the floor. The man began by telling Oliver he was a family man, with many children and grandchildren. Still, throughout his life, and in the jobs he'd held for more than forty years, he'd gotten by with the most meager of literacy skills. It was a secret he had harbored all his life with shame.

He was also a humble and devout churchgoer who attended regularly, he went on, always giving what he could to the collection plate. Now and then he even contributed his time to a variety of social events sponsored by the church. It was this last that threatened to expose his secret to the world.

The church elders, as they did every year, had organized a Christmas party for the children of parishioners. It was to be a festive gathering held in the church itself on the Sunday before Christmas, and which parents and church members were invited to attend. Gifts would be presented to the children, carols would be sung, and candies boxed in tins the shape of little churches would be given out. In addition, there would be special holiday selections read aloud to the assemblage by various selected members of the church.

This Christmas, the man explained to Oliver, he had been picked as one of those to speak. He had been asked to stand before his friends and neighbors on that Sunday afternoon and say words set before him on the piece of paper, words he knew he could not comprehend. Unable to decline for fear of acknowledging the truth, he'd started several weeks ago to try to teach himself to read. He began by making visits to a local library. But after several days, the librarian informed him that he was not welcome. She believed, she said, that he was actually a homeless person seeking shelter. She requested, further, that he leave the library and not return.

That was when he decided to come here to the Books section of the store. With the many customers and general activity at Christmastime, he hoped that he could pause unnoticed at the shelves and tables filled with books, and by looking at the words within them learn their meanings and the sounds they made.

And had he been successful? Oliver inquired.

Sadly, the man shook his head. True, he had learned some simple words. But not enough. It was now mid-December. The Christmas celebration at his church was drawing nearer, and the jumble of letters grouped together on a page was still almost as incomprehensible as it had always been.

The man stood up. "I'm sorry if I caused a problem. I'll go."

Oliver stood also. "I'd appreciate it if you stayed," he said. "Please wait one moment, if you would."

Oliver turned from the man and quickly rounded up the other clerks. Soon, the four of them approached the man again.

"I've spoken to my friends," Oliver said to him. "And we would very like you to continue coming here to Books."

Martha, Beatrice, and Roger nodded.

"Furthermore," Oliver went on, "we have a suggestion we would like to make. . . ."

On the Sunday afternoon preceding Christmas, in the pews nearest to the altar of the church, the children sat. The boys all wore suits, white shirts, and neckties; the girls, their best dresses, white stockings, and black shoes. Whispers of excited expectation filled the air. Behind the children sat their parents, friends, and others of the congregation, similarly murmuring their anticipation of the fete to come. Around the altar Christmas candles glowed, and bright red poinsettias adorned the aisles of the nave.

At exactly five P.M., the church organist struck up the chords of the processional; the congregation rose, and heads turned as the clergy and the church elders began their slow march down the aisle. . . .

Almost an hour later, the Christmas celebration neared its end. Several children recited poems they themselves had written, explaining in the simplest of words the wonder and significance of Christmas. Carols had been sung. The tins of candies had been handed out. Only one event remained—a special reading by a senior member of the congregation that would sum up the true spirit of the holiday itself.

It was the moment Oliver, Martha, Beatrice, and Roger had waited for. In a side pew in the last row of the church, the four of them sat side by side. Soon would come the moment all of them had worked so earnestly to make succeed.

At Oliver's suggestion, in the few weeks leading to this day, all had helped the man to read his piece. Each had taken turns when time permitted, sitting with him at a little table off the sales floor. They had begun with simple children's stories, sounding out the syllables and words as he repeated them. To their delight, they found him a receptive student, quick to learn, and like a starving man who finds a banquet set before him, insatiable in his hunger to learn more.

Now, at one side of the chancel, a door opened. Within the doorway stood the man. Heads turned in his direction. He, in turn, looked out at the congregation, squinting briefly at the brightness of the light. In his hand he held a sheet of paper. The paper trembled for an instant as the man walked to a lectern opposite the pulpit of the church. He stepped behind the lectern, placed the paper on it, smoothed it with a hand, and faced out toward the congregation once again. He bowed his head and briefly closed his eyes in prayer. At last he opened them. He took a breath. Then very slowly and deliberately, in a voice that carried to the farthest corners of the church, the man began to read:

"And it came—to pass—that there went out a—decree from Caesar—Augustus, that all the—world should be taxed. . . . And Joseph also went up from—Galilee . . ."

CHRISTMAS RAPPING

*F*irst a tone," Maude said.

She put the pitchpipe to her lips. In the cold air the note that flowed from it was pure and clear, despite the din of traffic and of people passing by.

"Aaah," sang Wilma.

"Aaah," repeated Beatrice.

The three young women stood together on the sidewalk at the southwest corner of the department store. Each of them was in her final year of study at the most prestigious music school in the city. Each was majoring in voice. Maude was a contralto, Beatrice and Wilma sopranos. Although Maude was small and a great deal shorter than her friends, she was the leader of the group. It had been her idea for the three of them to come that morning and to gather on the sidewalk near one of the store's entrances. There they would sing Christmas carols, a cappella style, to pedestrians and to the shoppers visiting the store.

Since Maude first suggested it, they had considered the idea for a week. They disliked the thought of being seen as street musicians, as some of their fellow students were—those who played classical selections on their violins in hope that passersby would drop some coins in the open violin case at their feet. If they sang, the three decided, it would be for the pure joy of singing without need of compensation, except for the acknowledged pleasure that it gave the crowd.

They had agreed on the repertoire the night before. They would begin with "Hark! The Herald Angels Sing!" a festive carol, and one sure to attract listeners. They would move on to the familiar favorites—"O Little Town of Bethlehem" and "Deck the Halls"; continue with some lesser carols, such as "Whence Comes This Rush of Wings"; and conclude with "Silent Night."

Now, Maude raised a hand. It fell decisively, and they began:

"Hark! The her-ald an-gels sing . . ."

Several people passing on the sidewalk stopped and looked at them. A woman smiled.

"Glo-ry to the new-born king! Peace on earth and mer-cy mild . . ."

Their voices melded in perfect harmony. More people stopped. A small group gathered. An old man in a mackinaw began to hum. A child clapped her hands together at her mother's side.

"Joy-ful, all ye na-tions rise—Join the tri-umph of the skies . . ." Wilma, Beatrice, and Maude sang out.

"Hey, man! How ya doing? . . . Gimme five! . . .

How you, brother?" The voices came from just around the corner of the store. A few shouts followed.

The three young women glanced at one another, but continued singing. Several in their audience looked furtively in the direction of the noise.

When the carol ended, the dozen or so people who had stopped to listen all applauded, then rapidly dispersed, rejoining the legion of pedestrians still flowing past.

The disruptive voices and shouting from around the corner were no longer heard.

" 'O Little Town of Bethlehem,' " Maude told the others, studying a list that she had brought. She added: "Key of G."

ADUMADUMADUMADUMADUM!

The pounding of a drum resounded just beyond the corner from which the voices and shouts had come. *ADUMADUM!*—Then suddenly the drumming stopped.

Maude frowned. "I'm going to see what all this is about."

Standing nearest to the corner of the three, Maude turned, inclined her head, and peeked around. She frowned again, and then withdrew.

"There's three of them. I saw them," Maude reported, whispering.

"Three of who?" Beatrice asked her.

"Three young men. Black."

"What are they doing?" Wilma pressed against the wall.

"Nothing," Maude said. "They're just standing talking. One of them is carrying a drum."

"Are they selling something?" Beatrice inquired. "Scarves or watches? Anything like that?"

"Not that I could see," Maude said.

"Maybe they're purse snatchers," Wilma offered. "There's lots of them around at Christmastime with everybody on the streets."

Maude considered this, but shook her head. "They don't look like purse snatchers. Of course, you can't be sure."

"Maybe we should move to another corner of the store," Beatrice said.

"The other corners are taken," Maude informed them. "There's a Salvation Army band at one, and Santa Clauses ringing bells at the two others."

"Maybe they're just passing by," Beatrice suggested hopefully. "Maybe they'll go on."

"Maybe," Maude said. "If not, we'll just ignore them. Once again, 'O Little Town of Bethlehem.'"

She raised her hand, and brought it down:

"*O lit-tle town of Beth-le-hem, How still we see thee lie! . . .*"

ADUMAUMADUMADUM! The drum sounded for a second time.

"Play it, daddy! Way to go!" Whoops and hollers echoed from around the corner even louder than before.

"Stop!" Maude waved her arms at Beatrice and Wilma. The singing of the carol ceased. The whoops and pounding of the drum did not.

"I'm going to speak to them," Maude said. She locked her arms across her chest, so that she looked like a small and rather angry bird. "I'll ask them to go somewhere else, so we can sing."

"Be careful," Wilma told her.

"We'll go with you," Beatrice said.

Together, the three young women moved toward the corner of the building. Maude was the first to round it, then Beatrice, and Wilma last. What they saw were three young black men just as Maude had said. The young men all wore jeans and leather jackets, with baseball caps turned backward on their heads. One was kneeling at a bongo drum, which he assaulted with a manic energy. Several feet away, his friends seemed to be doing some sort of dance, gyrating in place, heads down and bobbing, fingers snapping to the rhythm of the drum, as if caught up in a spastic trance.

"Uh . . . excuse me," Maude began.

"I don't think they can hear you," Wilma said in a low voice.

At that moment, the drummer turned his head in the direction of the women. "Whoa, brothers," he called to the dancers, keeping his eyes on the women the whole time.

"Excuse me," Maude repeated. "I'm very sorry to bother you. But I wonder—we wonder—if you and your friends would leave this corner. Please."

The drummer stood up slowly, cradling the drum under his arm. Standing before Maude, he was a full foot taller than she was, and very angular and thin. A small gem shone in his left earlobe.

"Huh?" he said to her. It sounded less a question than a grunt.

"It would help us if you'd move," Maude told him directly.

"Down the street, at least," Beatrice added quickly, so as to soften Maude's request.

"Why that?" the drummer asked.

"Because my friends and I would like to sing."

"That's what we gonna do. Sing."

"Rap," one of the dancers corrected him.

"This spot the three of us was at last week," the other dancer said. "How come we gotta move?"

"We like this spot," the drummer said.

Beatrice tried to give the young men a quick smile. "You see, we're studying singing at the music school. And we came here today—we're just around the corner, actually—in order to sing Christmas carols to people on the street."

The drummer smiled. "You sing carols. We sing rap," he told them. "You like rap?"

"Oh, rap music can be quite—inventive," Beatrice said.

"Know any rap carols?" he asked.

The other young men snickered.

"I think we better go," Wilma said to Maude.

Maude regarded the tall drummer. Then she nodded to her friends. "I guess we should." She turned and started toward the corner.

"Nice to have met you," Beatrice called cheerily over her shoulder as she hurried to catch up.

A short time later, after they had walked halfway around the store, Maude, Beatrice, and Wilma found a place next to another corner of the building, diagonally opposite from where they had first been. The Salvation Army band Maude had remembered from the day before was nowhere to be seen. Distantly, a Santa Claus's bell could be heard ringing, but it was too far away to cause the three concern.

"I think we'll be safe here," Maude said at last.

"Let's start again." She checked her list. " 'The First Noel.' " She raised her hand, and brought it down.

ADUMADUMADUMADUMADUM!

"It's *them*," Maude hissed. "They followed us."

"But we let them *have* their corner," Wilma said. She appeared close to tears.

"Street trash," muttered Maude. She thrust her hands into the pockets of her coat and marched in the direction of the sound.

Wilma looked at Beatrice. "They won't do something to her, will they?"

Quickly, the two hurried after Maude. Rounding the corner, they saw her flailing her arms in front of the tall drummer. He stared at her with half-closed eyes, as if he was extremely bored.

"You said that was your spot!" Maude's voice had taken a decidedly shrill tone. "We gave it to you!"

"Yeah. Well, now we got a new spot. Here." He pointed to the sidewalk. "The cops got on us where we was. So we moved here."

"How we know you gonna come here?" one of the other young men asked.

"All right," Maude said. "All right. If you insist on staying here, then so do we."

"And sing?" Wilma asked her.

"Of course we'll sing," Maude said. "Come on." She turned and started toward the corner, with Beatrice and Wilma close behind.

" 'Deck the Halls,' " Maude told them when they had returned to their side of the building. "Key of F." She raised a hand and quickly brought it down.

"*Deck the halls with boughs of hol-ly! . . . Fa-la-la-la-la—la-la-la-la . . .*"

The pounding of the drum began.

" 'Tis the sea-son to be jol-ly! . . ."

From around the corner now, the young men sang: "There's a great big hole in my Christmas stockin'! After Santa and his elves, they got me rockin'! . . ."

"Louder, girls! Fortissimo!" Maude shouted.

"Don we now our gay ap-pa-rel! . . ." the women sang full voice.

A few pedestrians slowed as they passed, regarding the young women with uncertain curiosity, then hurried on. Around the corner, too, the rappers' voices rang out.

"Bought a little Christmas tree, and then—you guessed it! The Man he came—and repossessed it!"

Countered the young women, "Troll the ancient yule-tide car-ol! . . . Fa-la-la-la-la—la-la-la-la . . ."

It was only during the last several "las" that the women realized the rap singing had stopped.

They looked around, surprised, and in so doing saw that the three young men had crossed to their side of the building and were standing there observing them, hands thrust in their jeans.

"Cool," the tall one said, when none of the young women spoke.

For the first time Maude seemed visibly uncomfortable. "What do you want now?" she asked. It was addressed to the drummer. Behind him she saw one of the other young men draw something shiny from his pocket. In his palm, there was the flash of metal glinting in the sun.

The young man read her face. "My bracelet," he told her. "I forgot to put it on." He clasped the bracelet on his wrist.

"You three sing good," the drummer told them. "Loud but good."

"Thank you," Wilma answered in a tiny voice.

"Why don't we sing together?" he said.

The woman looked at him.

"You mean the six of us?" Beatrice asked.

"Why not?"

"But your songs—" Wilma said. "I mean, our songs are Christmas carols. Everybody knows them. People have been singing them for years."

"Maybe they could use some bringing up to date," the drummer said.

At last Maude spoke. "Your rap songs may be up-to-date. But what about the words?"

"What about 'em?"

"Well, they're—"

"Dumb?"

"No, not exactly that. But—"

"I think a lotta fa-la-las is pretty dumb," the young man with the bracelet said.

"Any of you girls play piano?" asked the drummer.

"We all do," Wilma said.

"So you use the black keys and the white keys both together. Yeah?"

"Yes," Maude agreed.

"So," he went on, "you sing one of your songs and we'll sing one of ours to go along."

Beatrice looked puzzled. "You mean, you'll sing a rap song at the same time as we sing a Christmas carol?"

"You got it."

"No," Maude said. "We appreciate your suggestion," she informed the drummer. "But Christmas carols and rap songs wouldn't mix. They won't."

"How you know?" one of the young men asked.

Maude looked at him. "They wouldn't. I just know."

"We could try singing maybe one carol," Wilma said. "Their rap song could be like, well, counterpoint."

"What if we sang 'God Rest Ye Merry, Gentlemen'?" Beatrice offered.

Maude considered the idea. She looked at Beatrice, and then at Wilma, frowning as she did. Finally, she said, "We'll try. But only one."

" 'God Rest Ye Merry, Gentlemen.' " Maude raised a hand. "The key of E flat," she announced. The hand fell.

Sang the young women: "*God rest ye mer-ry gen-tle-men . . . Let no-thing you dis-may . . .*"

Sang the young men: "*Listen, everybody, it's the season of the yule . . . So even if they dis you, brothers, never lose your cool . . .*"

"*Re-mem-ber Christ, our savior, was born on Christ-mas day . . .*"

"*Think about the baby in the manger far away . . . Baby of a homeless two who had nowhere to stay . . .*"

And so the three young women sang their carol, and the young men rapped—as one by one those passing paused, and stopped to listen and to watch. For an hour, the six young people sang. Several times the crowd grew to such size around them on the sidewalk that pedestrians were forced into the street.

When the singing finally ended, and the last lingering member of their impromptu audience had gone, the young men and young women wished one another Merry Christmas. The young women then headed off in one direction, and the three young men the other.

It is unlikely they would ever meet again. That spring, presumably, the young women graduated from the music school and went forward in pursuit of their careers. What happened to the young men is not known. But for a brief time on that chill December day they sang together, celebrating Christmas in the way that each knew best, each voice adding to the chorus of rejoicing that was heard first from the voices of angels at a place called Bethlehem.

A MIRACLE
FOR MAX

*A*rnold Wembley was an actor. In all other respects he was a normal, reasonable human being; better than many, in fact. He was understanding of small children and of animals. On public transportation he unfailingly gave up his seat to pregnant women, the elderly, and the unfortunate. When he said "Please" and "Thank you," which was often, his sincerity was genuine. In some ways Arnie's physical appearance did not allow him to be other than the kind and gentle person that he was. Short and overweight, he had a bald head, large protuberant eyes, and wide lips that curved upward at the corners in an everlasting smile. Because of the impression Arnold Wembley gave the world, the acting roles he was cast in were usually the comic ones—the chump, the amiable blockhead, the buffoon.

This year, however, had been very difficult for

Arnie. His career seemed in decline. There were fewer roles he was asked to read for, fewer still which he won. His last employment four months ago in August had been as a fire hydrant in an avant-garde production staged in a converted tannery. The play closed after the second night.

Now it was mid-December and Arnie was in that state of anxious limbo actors euphemistically refer to as "at liberty." In short, he had no job; nor did there seem much possibility of finding one. As a result his finances were in desperate straits. Because he lived alone he had many times subsisted on the barest of necessities. With his inherent optimism, he had always comforted himself in the belief that soon a part would come along, or he would find temporary work outside of the theater, menial though it might be. But now when he went in search of employment, none of any sort was to be had.

What pained Arnie in particular was that he would have no money to buy Christmas presents for his sister's four young children. His sister had been widowed less than a year, and left with the two boys and two girls, none older than the age of eight. They lived in a tiny walk-up on the far side of the city. This was the first Christmas the children would be fatherless, and as much as Arnie had been the attentive uncle, and had helped to fill a certain void in their lives, he knew how difficult a Christmas this would be for all of them.

Several months ago, when he had had a little money, Arnie had vowed to buy Christmas presents for the children as the holidays approached. That time had arrived and the small savings Arnie had retained were just enough to see him to year's end.

Still, every day, in spite of the vagaries of the December weather, Arnie traveled about the city, hoping to find work. Often he would pass the great department store and envy the affluent shoppers he saw going in and out. Once, he even made a point of visiting the store himself. He went directly to the Toy section and picked out several toys with which he could surprise his nieces and nephews when he visited them Christmas Day. For little Anne Marie he chose a doll attired in a beautiful lace dress. For Will he found a model fire truck whose lights and siren looked and sounded like the real thing. For Sarah, who though only four was sure of her life's work, he got a doctor's kit. For her brother Tom, who was now reading everything in sight, he selected a young people's edition of the tales of King Arthur and his knights.

But when he brought the items to the register and the clerk totaled up the cost, the figure came to two hundred and sixty dollars and thirty-seven cents. Arnie blanched. He made a pretense of reaching in his pocket for his wallet. But he knew even before his fingers touched it that he had nowhere near that amount of cash.

He glanced up at the clerk sheepishly, and pushed the toys to one side. "I think I'll do more looking," Arnie lied. But he added, "I'll come back to the store another day." At the time, he had no idea how prophetic those words would be.

Arnie left immediately and returned home thoroughly depressed. That night he dreamed that he himself was Santa Claus, merrily dispensing to his sister's children all the toys he had found that day. In the dream the children laughed, and hugged and kissed him, and when he saw the smile on their mother's face as well as their smiles, it was the greatest Christmas gift he could have wished. Then the dream abruptly shifted. Suddenly, the *real* Santa Claus came through the window, seized the toys from the children's arms, and started out the door. But before exiting, he turned to Arnie. "Actor! Fake!" the spirit shouted at him. "Make something of yourself! Make money!" A moment later, Santa and the toys disappeared.

The next morning Arnie awoke shaken and even more discouraged than he'd been the day before. Although he felt no cheer within his heart, he affected the demeanor of the simple, happy man his actor's photographs portrayed, and headed out to make his rounds.

Still, as he went about the city, Arnie became aware of something he hadn't noticed until now. Perhaps the dream had prompted it. But as he walked along he saw a sidewalk Santa everywhere he looked. Of course, as Christmas Day approached their numbers multiplied. Yet there was no street anywhere he went that seemed without an imitator of the venerable old saint. Most of them had hand bells, which they rang to the accompaniment of ho-ho-hos, and all had cans or kettles into which they urged passersby to place their offerings.

Arnie wondered briefly if he, too, should try to get a job impersonating Santa Claus. He was as short as Santa, certainly, and ample at the waist. And though he had no beard or mustache—or, for that matter, much hair on his head at all—Arnie knew a costumer could furnish them, along with the red suit, hat, and high black boots.

But Arnie also knew a sidewalk Santa Claus made very little money. Some were even derelicts, seeking just enough for their next meal, or for a bottle or a bed. Pretending to be Santa was no way to amass a fortune,

Arnie told himself. In fact, he found it funny to imagine some of these red-suited impostors from the welfare rolls visiting a bank and building up a nest egg on the handouts they received.

That's when the idea struck him. It was so ingenious, so audacious, Arnie was amazed that nobody had thought of it before. He even grew a bit light-headed at its brilliance, so that he had to stop and lean against a nearby phone booth while he caught his breath. Looking in the booth, he saw that the telephone itself was missing, but a tattered phone book still hung down on a steel cord from where the phone had been.

Arnie stepped into the booth, picked up the phone book, and leafed through it quickly, searching for the address of a costume rental service he had sometimes used. Finding the address, he made a note of it.

Then Arnie smiled to himself. He knew what his next role as an actor would soon be. And he was determined to give it the performance of his life.

The following morning Arnold Wembley did not set out on his rounds. He did not hand out glossy photos of himself to any casting agents or producers' secretaries. He did not recite from memory his lengthy list of credits from the past.

Instead, as soon as he was sure the costume rental agency was open, Arnie went to it and rented for himself, for one day's use, a Santa Claus suit. He also rented a beard, a flowing white mustache, and a silvery white wig. The costumer's supply of Santa suits was limited, but to Arnie's great good luck they found one he could wear, even if the sleeves were somewhat long. He tried on the suit in one of the costumer's dressing rooms. Next, using a mirror on the wall, he put on the beard and mustache, then the wig, and above that the long red hat with the white pom-pom at the tip. Finally, he pulled on the black boots. A large white bag intended as a toy sack, for Santa Claus, was optional at a slight extra charge. But Arnie took it. Although toys were not what he would carry in the bag, he planned to put it to good use.

Half an hour later, dressed as Santa Claus and with the empty bag slung over his shoulders, Arnie started down the street where the bank that he had chosen stood. Yesterday he had crisscrossed the city searching for just such a bank as this. It was a small branch of a much larger financial institution. It appeared not to have too many customers at any given time. Most important, he had seen only one bank guard in evidence—a small, chatty older fellow in a uniform who hardly seemed the vigilant guardian of the bank's wealth.

Now, standing on the sidewalk facing the bank, Arnie questioned for the hundredth time if what he was about to do was right. For the hundredth time he told himself it was. He took a long, slow breath, then followed several people through the revolving door into the bank.

Just inside the lobby, he stepped to one side and accidentally bumped into a potted rubber plant. Opposite him, along the rear wall of the bank, was a long high counter behind which four women tellers stood, each transacting business for a customer. The bank guard, a man in his late sixties, stood beside the teller's station at the left, conversing amiably with the young and pretty teller as she went about her work.

The bank was very warm, and in his thick costume, Arnie found himself perspiring heavily. Nevertheless, he walked to the end of the line of eight bank patrons that wound circuitously through a course of metal stanchions. As each teller's station became free, the person at the head of the line would go to it. Arnie prayed that when his own turn came, fate would not direct him to the teller on the left where the guard stood.

Soon, there were seven customers in line ahead of him. Then six.

Surreptitiously, Arnie slipped a hand into a pocket of his Santa Claus suit. Good. The note was there. He had written it the night before on a small white slip of paper using a black felt tip pen. In block letters the note said PLEASE GIVE ME $260 IN SMALL BILLS. THANK YOU. He had decided against asking for the thirty-seven cents in change.

"Do you do this for a living?" someone asked.

Arnie turned behind him, startled. A short elderly woman with a cane was smiling at him.

"Do I do what?" Arnie said at last.

"Are you a Santa Claus for a department store? Or do you collect money on the street?"

"No, no—I'm an actor," Arnie told her.

"Really? Maybe I've seen you in something. What's your name?"

"Arnold—" he began, then stopped, realizing it would be unwise to give his actual full name, since in a few minutes he was about to rob the bank.

While the woman went on smiling, Arnie seized on the first name he could think of. "Benedict," he told her. "Arnold Benedict."

"Well, good luck, Mr. Benedict." She appeared very sympathetic. "Acting is a difficult profession."

Arnie nodded, thanked her, and turned forward again. Only three people stood in line in front of him. He was perspiring so profusely now that he could feel one corner of his mustache loosening. He raised a hand and pressed it to his face again.

Finally, a single customer, a young woman, stood between Arnie and the felony he would commit.

Scanning the four tellers' stations, he observed the station nearest to the guard was coming free; the young woman would go to it. Even better, Arnie thought, was that the teller at the opposite end of the counter would be free after that, and he would go to her.

Suddenly, the young woman ahead of Arnie looked into her open purse. "Oh dear, I forgot my checkbook. I'll have to come back another time."

"No, please. Don't go," Arnie pleaded. But the young woman had already stepped out of line, and was heading for the door.

"Next!" the bank guard called, and pointed to the teller's station next to where he stood.

Arnie's knees began to tremble and the light-headedness of yesterday returned. His black Santa Claus boots seemed frozen to the marble floor.

"You're next, Mr. Claus," the guard said cheerily.

Arnie felt the boots begin to move, propelling him in the direction of the teller's station on the left. Behind it, the pretty teller waited, smiling at the appearance that he made.

"Is this a deposit or withdrawal?" she asked Arnie.

" 'Drawal," he wheezed. "Cash."

The woman winked. "Do you need money for Mrs.

Claus's Christmas shopping or your own?" She gave a little laugh, as did the guard.

Arnie thought he was about to faint. The time had come. The moment was at hand, he told himself. It's now or never. Do or die. With that, he snatched the crumpled piece of paper from his pocket, placing it before her on the countertop.

"Make 'em crisp, huh?" Arnie mumbled.

"Merry Christmas to you, too," the teller said.

Then as Arnie watched, she began uncrumpling the piece of paper he had given her. She stared at it. A look of great perplexity ensued. Then she glanced over at the guard.

What happened next was a jumble. Arnie remembered turning from the teller, managing to cross the lobby, and then whirling around twice in the revolving door before being flung out onto the street. He recalled running—stopping—running—stopping more and more to catch his breath—then running again, having no idea what direction he was bound.

He had gone half a dozen blocks before he heard the siren. Quickly, Arnie stopped again and scanned the street. He didn't see any police cars, but the siren continued to grow louder.

Desperately, he checked the buildings nearest him to see if any offered sanctuary, somewhere he could hide. To his surprise he realized that he was on the sidewalk next to the department store. The main entrance was around the corner. Beyond him was the loading area from which trucks came and went, a set of doors for the employees, and a smaller metal door that was marked PRIVATE in small stenciled letters near the top.

At that moment a yellow school bus pulled up beside the curb. Its doors opened and excited children began pouring out. The children ranged in age from seven to about thirteen and were accompanied by a severe-looking woman who exhorted them with limited success to form themselves into a line.

Soon, the door marked PRIVATE swung out, and a security guard from the store appeared. As the guard held open the door, the severe-looking woman urged the children through it single file.

Closer came the siren—and in that moment Arnie knew what he must do. Dispensing hearty ho-ho-hos to no one in particular, he joined the line of children moving through the door.

"It's Santa! Santa Claus!" some children shouted when they saw him.

"Ho ho!" repeated Arnie, patting little heads around him as he pressed forward toward the door.

The children laughed and squealed, and those nearest Arnie reached out to touch his suit. The guard smiled, and even the woman tried to feign amusement. It was just as Arnie hoped.

The woman probably believed he was a store employee dressed up as Santa Claus; the guard must have thought he'd traveled with the children, and had also gotten off the bus along with them.

At last, everyone—the children, the woman, and the guard . . . and Arnie—were through the door and into a rear hallway of the store. The guard wished everyone a good time and a Merry Christmas, then stepped out the door onto the street, closing the door behind him as he went.

While the woman shepherded the children down the hall, Arnie slowed his steps, allowing them to gain some distance from him. When the woman and the children turned a corner and started down another hallway, Arnie didn't.

Instead, he stopped and looked around. The hall in which he stood was empty now except for him. At that moment, he heard the wail of the siren passing down the street outside where he'd been moments earlier. Gradually the siren faded, swallowed up by other traffic noises, until it could be heard no more. Arnie breathed a long deep breath.

He wondered what his course of action should be now. It then occurred to him that the department store was a huge place. It had dozens upon dozens of corridors and hallways just like this one. It had storage areas, and utility rooms used by the cleaning staff. And certainly, it had a basement; maybe even a subbasement where the machinery that furnished the store's basic services was housed. It would provide a perfect place to hide for a few hours. Then, later, he could reemerge from his subterranean concealment, slip out of the store, and mingle with the crowds.

Still studying the hallway where he stood, he noticed there were several other doors that faced along it. All were reinforced with metal, all had heavy hinges, some had dead bolts at the top and bottom. Arnie tried the doorknobs of a few of them, and found that they were locked.

Then, at the far end of the hall, he saw another door he hadn't observed earlier. Unlike the others, it stood narrowly ajar, propped open at the bottom by a thin wooden wedge.

Quietly, he tiptoed to it and peered in through the inch-wide opening. He saw nothing. Rather, it was what Arnie heard that made him think. He put his ear against the space and listened. From below came the deep whir and steady rumble of large pieces of equipment earnestly at work.

He eased open the door slowly. Then he stepped through it, closing it so that it came to rest against the wooden wedge once more. He discovered he was standing on a landing. Ahead, a set of metal stairs led downward. He waited until his eyes became accustomed to the meager light. Then, holding the railing with both hands, he leaned over and looked down. The stairway seemed to go on forever. Still, it seemed somewhat brighter at the bottom. Arnie started down.

After more steps than he had bothered counting, Arnie found himself standing on a concrete floor. Around him, illuminated by bare bulbs, he saw rows of massive steel pillars rising up into a latticework of pipes and ducts, crisscrossing in a labyrinthine maze. The noise of machinery he'd heard above now resonated all around him in a powerful deep roar. Combining to produce it were the mighty furnaces, the great turbines and air blowers, and the huge counterweights and cable housings of the store's elevators. Here, too, were the giant boilers sprouting their perplexities of gauges, dials, switches, valves, and curlicues of coiled copper pipes.

Remembering the brightly lit and fashionably decorated sales floors of the department store above, it was difficult for Arnie to imagine that this dim abyss was part of the same building. It appeared to be instead a shadowy and terrifying nether region populated by mechanical colossi.

Suddenly Arnie felt exceptionally tired. Nearby, leaning up against a pillar, was a short stepladder. Arnie unfolded it and eased himself down on it. Sitting there, hands resting on his knees, he had the feeling he was posing for a photograph.

But what an absurd picture it would be. And what would it be entitled? *Portrait of a Failed Actor, Failed Bank Robber, in a Rented Santa Claus Suit, Hiding in the Basement of a Large Department Store.*

Arnold Wembley wanted to cry. He was not self-pitying by nature. But he had never felt more foolish or inadequate than he did now.

Then Arnie heard the sound. He heard it even with the roar of the machinery. It was quite close, and came from just behind a boiler to his right. It was the scraping of a shoe against concrete. He stood up and listened hard. Could it be someone from the store's maintenance department who had come down to check on the equipment? Or could it be a guard who'd been alerted to his presence in the basement and was stalking him?

Whoever it might be, he thought, it was foolish of him to remain standing where he was. As gingerly as possible he moved in the direction of some huge motors that displayed a variety of winking lights. In the faint glow he could make out what seemed to be a line of wooden boxes, all of them large and piled up so as to form a wall. If someone else was down here, Arnie thought, the boxes would provide a perfect place to hide.

He reached the line of boxes and began to go around them—when he stopped. He stared.

Silhouetted in the low half-light was a small figure

facing him. It was a child, a girl about seven or eight. She was thin and small with dull dark hair cut short around her head. The clothes she wore appeared to be castoffs, discarded remnants people gave to charities; a child's loden coat with sleeves too short and several of the wooden buttons gone. Her slacks were denim, and her small black shoes were scuffed on every side.

"Who are you?" asked the child in a sharp high voice. "Are you from the store?"

"No." Arnie shook his head.

"Do you collect money on the street? Is that why you're dressed like that?"

"No," he repeated. By now, his initial fear had passed. Why this child should be in the basement, he had no idea. But in no way did she seem to be a threat.

"What are you then?"

"I'm Santa Claus," he told her. Play for time, thought Arnie. Humor her. He saw two smaller boxes sitting to one side and pointed to them.

"Look," he told the child with as much joviality as he could summon up. "I've been doing lots of traveling these days. And I'll do more on Christmas Eve. Let's sit down."

The child shrugged. But still she followed him. Arnie sat on a box facing her. "So, you know who I am," he said quickly. "Tell me who you are. What's your name?"

"Max."

"Max? That's a strange name for a girl."

"Maxine, really. But I hate it."

"Maxine is a very nice name," Arnie said.

"I hate it."

"Well—I'm surprised to find somebody down here."

"The others from the Home are up in toys. When Miss Rembock wasn't looking, I snuck off."

"What home is that? The place you live?"

"The Feldrick Home for Youth," the girl said. "Most are orphans, runaways. I live there 'cause my mother can't take care of me."

"I'm sorry," Arnie said.

"I'm not. She beat me up. That's why they put me in the Home. Anyway, before Christmas every year, they bring us here to see the toys. But I always sneak away and come down to the basement where it's quiet and there's nobody around." She looked at Arnie. "Till today."

"Why didn't you stay upstairs looking at the toys with the other children?"

"On account of if you see a toy you want, you're supposed to write Santa Claus a letter asking him to bring it."

"And you don't want to do that?"

"Why? That's stupid. That's for little kids. There is no Santa Claus."

Arnie looked down at the child's eyes. He did not see in them any of the mirth or innocence or expectation every other child he knew possessed at Christmastime. Instead all Arnie saw in them was disbelief, suspicion, and distrust. The sight made Arnie infinitely sad. And in that instant, he resolved to change it if he could.

"But *I'm* Santa Claus. I told you," he said softly.

"Yeah? How come you're down here in the basement then?"

"I'm lost. You see, every year about this time I visit

all the toy sections in the world to see what children want. . . ."

She moved her mouth to one side, but said nothing.

"I was just leaving the department store," Arnie went on, "when I took a wrong turn, and discovered I was here instead of on the street."

"That's where you left your sleigh?"

"Yes. No . . ." Arnie paused. He was perspiring heavily again. "Actually, my sleigh and reindeer are inside a big truck parked around the corner. After I leave here, I'll drive the truck out into the country where nobody can see it. I'll unload the sleigh and reindeer, and fly back to the North Pole."

"What about the truck? Did you hijack it?"

"I didn't hijack it. It's mine. My helpers drive it back."

"Who are your helpers? Elves?"

"Some are. Some aren't. A few are midgets, actually. They don't have magic powers like the elves, but they're good workers."

For the first time there was a smile on the child's face. "You know what, Santa Claus?" she said.

He smiled back. "What, Max?"

"I think you're full of it. I think you're just a fat man in a Santa suit."

Arnie said nothing. His natural fondness for young people in general had diminished swiftly in the presence of this child. But as flip and streetwise as she seemed, he was determined to try one more time.

He leaned forward toward her. "Tell you what," said Arnie. "You don't believe I'm Santa Claus."

Max shook her head. "Why should I?"

"Because Santa Claus has special powers. Magic

powers. And if I'm really Santa Claus, I should be able to do miraculous things. Do you know what a miracle is?"

The child thought. "It's things that happen that you can't explain."

"That's right," he told her. "And suppose I could do something here today that couldn't be explained. Would you believe that I was Santa Claus then?"

"It depends on what you did." Her expression remained skeptical. But her tone showed she was intrigued.

"Well, let's see." Arnie shoved his hands into the trouser pockets of his Santa Claus suit to think. By chance, his right hand touched some coins. It gave him an idea. Several years ago he'd played the part of a magician's helper in a magic show and learned some simple tricks.

"Okay, okay," he said. He waved his left hand with a dramatic flourish, while he grasped a quarter in his pocket with the right. Lifting the right hand unobtrusively, and bending it, the quarter slid up inside his sleeve.

"Observe. . . ." He stepped to her and waved both open hands before her face, chanting in his best magician's voice.

"Donner and Blitzen and all my reindeer . . . I can make money come out of your ear!"

He placed his right hand close to her ear as the quarter dropped into his palm. He held it pressed between his thumb and forefinger and removed his hand with it to show her.

"Ta-da! Behold!" He flipped the quarter in the air. "A miracle!"

"That's not a miracle. The quarter came from your pants pocket. Then you put it in your sleeve."

"Of course I did!" His hearty laugh surprised her. "I was just testing you to see how smart you were. And you are one smart little girl."

Arnie sat down on the box again. "Listen, Max. Let's make a deal. If you help me get out of here without anybody seeing me, I'll personally bring a Christmas present to you at the Home. What do you say?"

Max abruptly stood. "So long, Santa. That's what I say." She began to walk away.

"Where are you going? . . . Max?"

She ignored him, quickening her step.

He started after her. "Hey, wait a minute, Max!"

Ahead, she turned and headed down a passageway between wire cages housing large equipment. Arnie started down the passageway.

Finally, he stopped and called out, "Max!"

Then behind him Arnie heard a sound. He turned around and found he was confronting a brick wall about six feet from where he stood. The sound appeared to come from the wall itself. What he heard was a low cooing. He put a hand against the wall and moved quietly in the direction of the sound, feeling with his hand along the bricks.

His fingers suddenly touched empty space. Moving both his hands he found there was a round opening, about a foot wide and at shoulder height. He guessed that it was where a pipe had once been placed, and then removed. Arnie put his face against the opening. What he saw was a small pigeon. Against the blackness it appeared almost completely white. How the bird got here was a mystery. Somehow it must have wandered or fallen accidentally into an open pipe or air duct and couldn't find its way back out. The pigeon turned and looked at Arnie. As if greeting him, it blinked and bobbed its head.

Arnie reached into the opening, took the pigeon quickly with both hands, and brought it to him. He could see now that the bird was very young. It showed no sense of fear. Instead, it sat docilely in his hands, pecking curiously at a button of his Santa suit.

With a finger, Arnie stroked the soft feathers of the bird's small head and back. Then, still clutching it against his chest, he started up the passageway again.

"Max—where are you? Look what—"

Arnie stopped. He moved the bird to one of the vast side pockets of his Santa Claus coat and slipped it down inside. Now he stepped into the lighted aisle.

"Max?" he called again. "I've got something to show you!"

To his surprise the child appeared from behind the pillar opposite the place he stood.

"Is it another miracle?" Max said.

"This time I think it is."

Arnie removed his Santa Claus hat, turned it upside down, and held it out to her. "Look inside my hat. Tell me what you see."

She stepped toward him and peered into the hat reluctantly.

"Do you see anything?"

"No."

"Now put your hand inside it. Do you feel anything?"

Warily, she placed an arm down in the hat and felt around.

"Is the hat empty?"

She withdrew her arm and nodded. "Yes."

"Watch this."

In a single swift motion, Arnie swept the hat along the side of his coat, at the same instant scooping the bird out of the pocket with one hand and depositing it in the hat. Again, he held out the hat in her direction.

"Now look."

The child bent forward and looked down. As she did, her face was transformed from skepticism to astonishment. "It's a bird," Max whispered. "Is it real?"

"Certainly it's real."

Arnie lifted the baby pigeon from his hat and offered it toward her. "Would you like to hold it?"

"Can I?"

"Give me your hands."

Slowly, the child cupped her hands together and extended them in his direction, her eyes fixed on the bird. With great care Arnie placed the bird within them. Her fingers closed around the small white creature and she brought it to her chest, still looking down at it in awe.

"Is this the miracle you promised?"

"What do you think?"

She didn't answer. Finally, she met his eyes. "I don't know."

Arnie smiled. "Well, that's just how it should be with miracles. Some people believe in them, and some don't. And some people aren't sure. If everyone believed in them every time they happen, then they wouldn't be miraculous. Miracles should always leave you wondering."

He bent down so that he faced the child. "Now, how about it? Will you help me to get out of here?"

She continued looking at the little bird. "Okay," she told him. "Follow me."

She turned from him, still holding the bird close to her, and started off. Her route led among large pieces of machinery, and Arnie had to hurry to keep up. Momentarily, she disappeared from view. When he caught sight of her again, she was waiting for him at the bottom of a narrow stairs.

"I'll go first," she said as he arrived.

She mounted the stairs, carrying the bird in both hands. Arnie lumbered up behind her, one hand clutching the rail, not daring to look down.

As he reached the topmost step, Max eased aside a door. She put her head into the opening, then waved for him to follow.

Arnie stepped out through the door—and discovered he was standing on the street.

He blinked his eyes against the light. "Where are we?"

"Around the corner from the store," Max said. She made a wry face. "Do you think you can find your way to the North Pole from here?"

"I think so," he said. "And you better get back to the store."

She nodded, frowning. "Yeah." She glanced down at the little bird. "First, though, I better let it go. They don't let us keep pets at the Home."

Arnie placed a hand lightly on the child's head and smoothed her hair. "Well, a bird this young must have a mother nearby. If you let it go then it can fly to her."

"That'd be nice," Max said. "I hope her mother loves her all the time, and never hurts her."

"Oh, she will," he assured the child. "She'll love her very much."

The child closed her eyes and pressed the bird to her again for a brief moment. Then she raised her arms above her head and with a sudden upward thrust released it. The bird faltered, flapping rapidly, then lifted, rose, and rose still higher, reaching for the sky.

The following is a chronology of disparate events, which though they may seem unrelated in some instances, provide a necessary coda to this story. . . .

A short time later, the group of children visiting the Toy section of the store that day reboarded their bus and departed for the Feldrick Home for Youth. Among them was a small, dark-haired girl in a loden coat.

Throughout that same week, the employees of a small bank near the department store remained puzzled over an incident that had occurred a few days earlier. A short fat man had entered the bank dressed in a Santa Claus suit. As he approached the teller, he had wished her Merry Christmas, and then placed a piece of paper down in front of her. The paper, it turned out, was a receipt from a costume rental company for a day's rental of a Santa suit, presumably the one worn by the man himself. The teller was about to question him concerning it when the man abruptly turned and fled the bank.

That week also Arnold Wembley was hired for an acting job. It was as a talking reindeer, entertaining children outside a suburban mall, but it paid reasonably well. What's more, by the most serendipitous of circumstances, he was spotted in that role by a film producer, who immediately cast him in a lavish movie epic the producer planned.

Indeed, Arnie's fortunes changed so swiftly that on Christmas Day he went to the apartment of his sister bearing gifts for her and for her children just as he had hoped—a doll for Anne Marie, a fire truck for Will, a doctor's kit for Sarah, and a book for Tom.

Yet before going there, Arnie made another visit first. It was to the Feldrick Home for Youth. At the front desk, and without giving his name to the receptionist, he left a large and beautifully wrapped present for a child he knew only as Maxine. The present was a new and handsome loden coat of finest quality, plus a pair of colorful wool slacks, and black patent leather shoes, all in a child's size. The note attached said simply, "For Max—with special love and Christmas greetings always."

It was signed: "Your friend from the basement of the department store—S. Claus."

THE TWELVE
SHOPPING DAYS
OF CHRISTMAS

TO: Mr. William Whitaker
FROM: Ms. M. Chase
RE: Personal Shoppers' Service

12 December

Dear Sir:

We are in receipt of your inquiry to the department store concerning shopping services for discriminating customers, who, for whatever reason, are unable to make their desired purchases themselves.

For these people, such as yourself, the store's Personal Shoppers' Service was created. My name is Ms. Chase, and I have been assigned to assist you in securing the items you request.

As you know, this store carries the broadest selection of merchandise. Nevertheless, if an item should be unavailable we will make every effort to obtain it from another source. Once that is done, we will arrange for its delivery to you.

Beginning tomorrow, December 13, there are only twelve shopping days remaining before Christmas. Therefore, in order to locate and dispatch the items you request, we ask that you send a list of them in writing to me, as your personal shopper, using the fax number of the Personal Shoppers' Service noted at the bottom of the page. I will acknowledge your request, also by fax, and provide you with any information that concerns your purchase.

Again, the Personal Shoppers' Service is delighted that you have called upon us to assist you in your holiday selections.

Respectfully,
Ms. Chase

13 December

Dear Sir:

This is to confirm your message of this morning. As I understand it, the twelve orders you intend to place with us will be given as gifts to your fiancée. For that reason you ask that they be sent to you as soon as possible. There will, of course, be an additional delivery charge for same-day service.

Now to your order—and may I say, what a perfect gift to give someone at Christmastime! Although the department store does not maintain a garden shop or nursery where live plants are sold, our Decorative Accessories section has an adorable little imitation pear tree complete with carved, hand-painted pears. As for the accompanying gift, a partridge, the manager of Sporting Goods is a licensed taxidermist, and just happened to have a stuffed partridge on display. He was reluctant to part with it. But since you said money is no object, he agreed.

Both the pear tree and stuffed bird should reach you by this afternoon.

Sincerely,
Ms. Chase

14 December

Dear Mr. Whitaker:

I'm delighted that the tree and partridge arrived safely. How sweet of you to make a little ceremony of presenting them to your fiancée, and that she called you her "true love."

Your second request, however, was something of a challenge. Since you indicated you would prefer real birds to stuffed ones, I contacted a pet store in the neighborhood, and was pleased to find they carried turtle doves. I think you'll find the two doves make a lovely cooing sound together. The bird cage is a bit ornate, but it can be exchanged.

I am also taking the liberty of sending with your order a bag of birdseed at no extra cost.

Very sincerely,
Ms. Chase

Dear Mr. Whitaker:

I certainly hope your fiancée likes birds! And that she has a place to keep the new bird cage containing the three French hens.

Thank you, by the way, for your compliments regarding what you called my "resourcefulness" in finding just the gifts you want. The fact is, Mr. Whitaker, this is my first real job. But I'm determined to see to it that your purchases are pleasing to you—and of course, to your fiancée—so that they may add joy to the holiday for both of you.

Most sincerely,
M. Chase

16 December

Dear Mr. Whitaker:

Oh dear. Did one of those French hens actually turn out to be a rooster? I do apologize, and also blush at the thought of what your fiancée discovered when she looked into the cage!

At least, I'm glad you told me that she's interested in ornithology, which helps explain today's gift of four calling birds. Let me add quickly that not everyone considers the macaw to be a "calling bird." But the supplier of exotic animals who sold them to me said the squawks are really love calls. And they *are* pretty, don't you think?

With good wishes,
M. Chase

17 December

Dear Mr. Whitaker:

Well, the five gold rings from our Fine Jewelry department should please her, and, I hope, help to change the foul mood she's in because of the macaws. I'm sorry if their constant screeching didn't let her get a wink of sleep last night.

Many good wishes,
M. Chase

18 December

Dear Mr. Whitaker:

So the rings restored peace between the two of you! I'm glad. Of course, the six geese I'm sending today aren't exactly quiet birds. But the poultry man from whom I got them promised they'll lay lots of eggs. I hope you and your fiancée like omelets.

Best wishes,
Melanie Chase

19 December

Dear Mr. Whitaker:

I regret the mess those goose eggs must have been for both of you. If I had been your fiancée, however, I would have used a word other than *bizarre* to describe your gifts to her. I find them quite unique. And most important, it's the thought that counts.

My very best,
Melanie Chase

P.S. I hope today's gift to her of seven swans is without problems. (Or should I say, doesn't lay an egg?) I'll be thinking of you.

20 December

Dear Mr. Whitaker:

Your description of the fight sounds simply terrible—the fight between the geese and swans, I mean; not the one between you and your fiancée. I can imagine all those feathers flying in the air.

Concerning your order of today, I hired the eight maids through a listing in the yellow pages for Maid Services. The cows come from an upstate farm. Although they're somewhat old (the cows, that is, not the maids), I'm told they're still good milkers.

As for the postscript to your note to me, I'm touched and honored that you find me the friendliest, most helpful salesperson you have ever met—or in this case, haven't met. And I agree. Since we've been communicating for a week, the use of our last names seems overformal. So I'll call you William from now on, and you can call me Melanie. About your second question—how would I describe myself? Let's see. I'm twenty-two years old, tall, with long dark hair and hazel eyes. Some friends say I should go into modeling, but I enjoy helping people so much, this is the perfect job for me. Especially when I have wonderful customers like you.

Thank you again for your compliments.

Melanie

21 December

Dear William:

Nine ladies dancing? I'm sure you thought you had me stumped this time. With all the ballet groups busy in holiday performances, I couldn't get a single prima ballerina, much less any girls from the corps de ballet, to come and dance for you today.

Then I remembered the club where my ex-boyfriend and I used to go. Last night I went there by myself and in no time at all had hired nine female dancers straight off the dance floor. Some of them aren't exactly "ladies," if you get my meaning. But they certainly can dance! You'll see.

Cha cha cha,
Melanie

22 December

Dear William:

Dancing is dancing, as you say. So I'm sorry for you that your fiancée wasn't more forgiving when she showed up unexpectedly and discovered you doing the lambada with the dancing ladies.

With sympathy and understanding,
Melanie

P.S. Before I forget, let me tell you about what, or rather who, will be arriving at your door this afternoon. They call themselves the Lords. They're a semi-pro basketball team, particularly noted for their ability to leap. Between the five regulars and five subs, that makes the ten leaping lords that you requested. Since they're scheduled to play tonight, I regret they'll only be able to give you and your fiancée a short intersquad game.

23 December

Dear William:

Forgive this brief message, but with only two days until Christmas, we're swamped with scads of orders.

The eleven bagpipers who will appear today are from the police department's Emerald Society. (Aren't they cold wearing kilts in late December?) I hope their bagpipes don't freeze up.

As always,
Melanie

24 December

Dear William:

Bagpipe music is an acquired taste, I'm sure. And I can understand it if the eleven pipers piping gave your fiancée a migraine. Still, after all these days in which you've showered her with gifts, it seems ungrateful at the very least for her to call you a jackass and a fool.

Her unappreciative behavior makes me wonder even more about your gift to her today—twelve drummers drumming. If it's any help to you, you can assure her that the drummers are all members of the best musical organizations I could find. They come from the philharmonic orchestra, several military drill teams, and a rock band.

One final note. Since this is the last message I will fax to you, I wanted you to know that I've come to think of you as a friend, and not merely as a customer. And although we've never met, I also like to think I've come to know you and admire you for the romantic ways in which you've endeavored to bring Christmas to your fiancée.

Tomorrow I'll be thinking of you, and wishing you (and her) a very Merry Christmas.

Melanie

24 December (4:30 P.M.)

Will—

What a wonderful surprise! A few minutes ago your lovely note showed up on my fax machine, along with the picture of yourself. You're even handsomer than I imagined! And is that huge house behind you in the photo really yours?

I'm sorry, by the way, to hear about you and your fiancée. But honestly, after the problems that the two of you have had I'm not surprised. Even so, for her to run off with the drummer from the rock band is a heartless way to treat the kind and generous person who I know you are.

Believe me, Will, I *do* appreciate how lonely you must be today, even with the other eleven drummers still sitting in your kitchen drinking up the eggnog that you made. Therefore, I'll be pleased to join you tomorrow, Christmas Day, to share the dinner that you planned for you and your fiancée.

I ask only one favor of you. Please don't give me any gifts.

Love,
Mel

Why then do I beg......of when I write it for my eyes alone? The truth is... do so to search my being and in this account to make a record of my life, such as

THE STAR CHECKER

"Jimmie" the name read, stitched in light green thread above the left-hand pocket of his work shirt. But it and the others Jimmie wore had been laundered so many times over the years that the name was barely visible against the dark green fabric of the shirt itself. His full name was James Francis Xavier Bright, although everyone on the maintenance staff of the department store always called him Jimmie. Out of Jimmie's hearing a few of the brash younger ones disparaged him as the Old Man. But even they remained respectful of the seniority Jimmie Bright had earned.

It was known that he was well into his eighties. How well into them nobody was sure. Even people meeting him for the first time were hard put to know his age. They would admire the full head of gray-white hair and the thicket of eyebrows, also gray, beneath his brow.

They would detect the subtle slope of the broad shoulders. Standing close enough, they'd note the emerald eyes framed by tortoiseshell glasses. Looking at his hands they would observe the greatly callused palms, and on top, the skein of bulging bluish veins. Even then, they'd guess him to be in his late seventies. And they'd be wrong.

Today, however, Jimmie felt his age. It was a morning in the middle of December. The atmosphere within the store was warm and cheerful, but on the streets outside a chill rain fell. Jimmie's spirit matched the bleakness of the day.

He stood in the broad center aisle of the store's main floor. Shoppers hurried past, a rolling stock cart rumbled near him, carols wafted on the air. At the far end of the aisle, crowds of children chattered, pointing at the exquisitely decorated Christmas tree surmounted by a crystal star.

Jimmie Bright paid no attention to the shoppers, or the rolling stock cart, or the children ringed around the tree. What he was studying instead was one darkened glass globe in a row of lighted globes that hung down from the ceiling near where Jimmie stood. He lifted the clipboard he was carrying, withdrew a wooden pencil from the pocket of his shirt, and on the pad attached to the clipboard noted:

"Main floor—third hanging ceiling light from left of Millinery counter—burned-out bulb inside globe—(150 watts)."

The bulb itself could not be seen, of course, but Jimmie knew its wattage from the many times he'd changed them in the fixtures through the years.

Yet Jimmie would not change this bulb or any other

in the store again. The task to which his supervisor had assigned him for the day was to walk through the aisles and the halls, eyes focused upward, making note of any lights that might have failed, or were in the flickering last hours of their lives. At no time was he to attempt to change the bulbs, the supervisor said. Just note the location, and if possible the wattage of the bulb, and another man would be dispatched to change it when he could.

"That's all?" Jimmie Bright had asked the supervisor. "Look out for dead light bulbs?"

"It's an important job," the man had answered with an enthusiasm Jimmie didn't share. The supervisor had then handed him the clipboard and the pencil, and gone off.

"Dead bulbs," said Jimmie to himself. "It's come to that."

How different it had been when he first came to the department store so many years ago. Even the great store itself was different then. The cash registers were large contraptions in those years, ratchety and hand cranked, nothing like the sleek sophisticated models of today. In those years, messages and sales slips were shot pneumatically about the store in ganglia of metal tubes. In those years, elevators weren't sterile boxes with Formica walls, but ornate, bird cage–like conveyances of filigreed design that floated gracefully from floor to floor.

The Jimmie Bright who'd found employment within the walls of the department store had been a personable lad of twenty, eager then to take on any job he was assigned. He had a ready smile, and in the company of the other men of Maintenance, an honest friendliness that had earned him their affection and support. And he was strong—Young Samson several of them called him. Were there elevator cables needing to be pulled by hand? Ask Jimmie. Did a frozen joint in a pipe resist repeated efforts of a Stilson wrench to set it free? Get Jimmie Bright.

With his mane of jet-black hair and sparkling green eyes, he was a favorite of the women working in the store as well. Still, there was one who captured his heart almost at once. Her name was Mary; she was Jimmie's age, and very pretty in a fragile sort of way. Mary was employed by the cleaning staff. Within a year of meeting one another they were married. Soon, four children followed: three boys and a girl. As his young family flourished, Jimmie had never been more happy in his life. Then swiftly, grievously, pneumonia claimed the life of his dear Mary. For a full week Jimmie Bright was absent from the store. When he returned, he threw himself into his work with even greater zeal, most said as a palliative for his pain and loss.

Years passed. Despite the many women who would have gladly sought the role of his wife and mother to his children, he did not remarry. Jimmie raised the children by himself, trying to the best of his ability to guide and nurture them as Mary would. And day after day, year upon year, he went about his job in Maintenance. He gained such a reputation with his fellow workers they were certain no problem was beyond him. There was no piece of equipment that he couldn't fix; no faltering machine, whatever its complexity, that he could not repair.

Yet there was one complicated mechanism on which the accumulated years of wear were irreversible. And that was Jimmie Bright himself. As he aged into his sixties, certain jobs he'd always done were taken from his hands; responsibilities he'd held for years became the work of other, mostly younger, men. Employees of the department store, on reaching sixty-five, were no longer obligated to retire. But most did, choosing to enjoy time with friends and families, or to pursue personal endeavors of their own. When Jimmie Bright reached sixty-five he thought about retiring, and rejected it. With Mary gone and all his children grown and scattered to the winds, the work he did in Maintenance was Jimmie's life. Retire? Not while he had strength enough to do the tasks assigned.

So through his sixties, and on into his seventies—no matter that his eyesight had diminished, that his joints sometimes cried with pain, or that he couldn't climb a flight of stairs without a pause, his hand held to the railing, Jimmie Bright continued coming to the store.

Then a month ago, the floor tile incident occurred. Jimmie had been kneeling in a hallway off the sales floor, replacing squares of vinyl tiling, when a wave of dizziness assaulted him. He dropped the tile he was holding and put both hands on the floor. The next thing he remembered was the ambulance attendant bending over him and pressing something large across his face. A case of vertigo, the doctor in the hospital explained. It happened now and then, he said, to older people Jimmie's age.

The morning of the day that he reappeared in Maintenance, the supervisor and the others welcomed him with friendly words. A few men slapped him on the back. But in their greetings, and despite their jovial assurances that they were glad to have him on the job again, he noted in their eyes a certain doubt he should have returned at all.

It was after the brief welcome had concluded, and

the men of Maintenance had gone their ways, that Jimmie read the sheet listing his assignments for the week:

Monday (it said): Visit rest rooms. Look for faucet drips. Replace washers where needed. . . .

Tuesday: Remove bent nails from nail boxes on carpentry shelves. Straighten nails or discard (Put screws in a separate can). . . .

Wednesday: Check all lights in store for burned-out bulbs. . . .

Jimmie had stared down at the sheet, rereading it a second time, and then a third. They were the most menial, the most demeaning, tasks he'd ever been directed to perform.

Still, all during Monday Jimmie bent in front of every rest room sink, his eyes alert for faucet drips. On Tuesday, he picked over several thousand nails, straightening each one that was bent. At no time did he say anything to anyone about how deep a wound his pride had suffered, how much loss of self-respect he'd undergone.

By late Tuesday afternoon, however, his hurt was so apparent that two of his friends decided something must be done. First thing Wednesday morning, before Jimmie headed out about the store to check for burned-out bulbs, his friends, together with some other men in Maintenance, staged an informal ceremony. One of them made a short speech, full of humor and goodwill, in which he said that checking light bulbs was a far more important task than Jimmie thought. Not only was it his job to look at all the ceiling lights, but now with Christmas drawing near, he had the great responsibility of overseeing every row of Christmas lights the store had strung to complement the holiday decor. In fact, the man insisted, Jimmie shouldn't think of them as Christmas lights at all. He should consider them as stars. From that day forward, Jimmie would be known to them as the Star Checker. No one else they knew could do the job.

The speech ended. Everyone applauded, and a few slapped Jimmie on the back again.

Jimmie thanked them. The Star Checker. At least it had an important-sounding ring to it, he said. Then he picked up his clipboard, put the pencil in the pocket of his shirt, and started for the service elevator that would take him to the main floor of the store.

By five o'clock that evening he had covered every floor of the department store. Beginning on the main floor, he had worked his way up to the top where the offices of the executives were found. On that floor, every light bulb Jimmie checked, whether in the offices themselves or in the halls, was burning brightly, which he considered a good omen for the store's success.

He then descended one floor to the section that sold rugs. In Rugs, he found a long fluorescent that no longer illuminated several stacks of dhurrie carpeting. In Lamps, a faulty filament inside a table lamp did not escape his gaze. In Girls/Boys 4–7, Jimmie saw at once a spotlight that was dimmer than it ought to be. This, too, was recorded on his clipboard pad.

But it was the rows of Christmas lights strung beneath the ceilings of the sales floors to which he paid particular attention.

The Star Checker, he repeated to himself as he moved throughout the store that day. His friends in

Maintenance had meant the title as a joke. Yet as he walked from floor to floor, eyes focused upward on the galaxies of tiny lights, he found himself imagining they *were* stars, real ones, and that they all were his responsibility—and his alone—to keep alight.

It was at that moment Jimmie Bright decided what he had to do. Before he went off duty for the night he would seek out his supervisor and request that he be made official Star Checker for the store. The job gave meaning, purpose, to his life again; although he decided not to tell his supervisor that. Instead, he'd simply volunteer that in addition to his other duties, he would make a daily circuit of the store, inspecting every strand of ornamental Christmas lighting, and make certain each one of the little bulbs was lit.

The elevator was nearby, so Jimmie went to it. He had descended several floors when he discovered it was not the service elevator he had meant to board, but one of those reserved for customers. As the car stopped at each floor, crowds of people bearing shopping bags poured into it, and Jimmie was pressed farther to the rear. When the car arrived at the main floor he exited it with the crowd. The service elevator was across the floor, so Jimmie turned and started down the central aisle heading toward it.

He had walked only a short distance when he realized that something was not right. He stopped and looked around. Customers still filled the aisles. Many crowded at the counters. What had made him stop?

Then, facing him, no more than twenty feet away, he saw the Christmas tree that was the centerpiece of the main floor of the department store. Reaching to the ceiling and elaborately decorated, it was seen by all who visited the store each year at Christmastime. Always, they exclaimed over its beauty. But for Jimmie Bright it had even greater meaning. Every year, until this one, he'd been among the men from Maintenance who'd help erect the tree, and had assisted the trimmers from the decorating staff in stringing the long rows of lights and hanging the hundreds of beautifully crafted ornaments along the boughs.

Yet now as Jimmie slowly raised his eyes from bough to bough, he knew what he had sensed that made him stop. The light that always shone within the crystal star atop the tree was dark.

How could he have missed it earlier? The star was probably the most visible and most admired object in the store throughout the holidays. The glass was of the finest European crystal, with long delicately tapered points like the Star of Bethlehem that had led the shepherds and the Wise Men to the manger where the Baby Jesus lay.

Jimmie lowered his eyes. Then he took the pencil from his shirt pocket, raised the clipboard, and wrote on the pad:

"Main floor—Christmas tree in center aisle—Bulb inside the crystal star at top burned out. . . ."

He was about to add what he was certain was the wattage of the bulb—or should be. In the past it had been Jimmie who had installed a new bulb every year before the star was lit. But this year the assignment had been given to a new man on the staff, a fellow he knew had not the same affection for the tree that he had. Obviously, the bulb the man had placed inside the star had failed. Had the man tested it beforehand? Did he care that others, even Jimmie himself, had sometimes looked up at the light it gave and felt a sense of hope when hope seemed lost?

He knew the answer. And at that moment Jimmie Bright also knew what he must do.

It was well after nine o'clock that night when he returned to the department store. Once in, he took the service elevator down to Maintenance. Three men from the night staff were on duty at that hour. Two of them were playing cards; a third man read a book. As he entered, the card players raised their eyes in brief acknowledgment, then went back to their game. Not one of them noticed Jimmie as he took a light bulb from the shelves that housed electrical supplies. Nor did they see him hoist the tall stepladder on his shoulder and depart.

A short time later the ladder stood beside the Christmas tree. Except for Jimmie there was no one on the floor. The cleaning crews had come and done their work and gone, and the guard from night security was not due to pass this way for half an hour.

Jimmie eased the ladder closer to the tree, so that its lowest steps were nestled in the branches at the base, and rocked it gently from one side to the other to make certain its feet were squarely on the floor. Then Jimmie stepped away and looked up at the tree again. Tears began to fill his eyes, and with them memories came flooding back. That first Christmas after he and Mary had been wed, they'd stood together by the tree and shared the joy that the sight of it evoked. The Christmas after she had died, he'd come again at night to gaze at it, alone and trying to assuage his grief.

Now, holding the ladder on both sides, he lifted one foot and placed it on the bottom step. The other soon joined it.

Slowly, he moved to the second step. . . . Then to the third. . . . And up he moved, past gleaming colored balls and airy angel hair spun out like gossamer. . . . Past ornaments that danced and twirled; elves and cherubs, winged swans and leaping deer, and dashing Santa Clauses in their sleighs. . . . Past rows of tiny colored lights, all twinkling, that wound around the tree.

The task was simple, Jimmie told himself; he'd done it many times before. Reach out. Remove the crystal star. Exchange the old bulb with the new. Replace the star.

Another step. . . .

Another. . . .

. . . Until Jimmie Bright stood on the very top. Then, arms extended; fingers spread; with joy, trust, and infinite serenity—as if he were about to take the hands of God Himself—he touched the crystal star. . . .

At nine-thirty P.M. the body of James F. X. Bright was discovered by the night guard making his scheduled visit to the floor. The old man was lying face up at the base of a tall ladder that had been placed beside the giant Christmas tree. Other guards were summoned. The police arrived, and then a coroner, and after all of the forensic facts were noted, the body was transported to the office of the medical examiner in order to determine cause of death.

On the day after the accident the supposition was

that Jimmie Bright had been the victim of a sudden massive heart attack. The man was old, after all. Yet Jimmie's face showed not the slightest evidence of pain. To the contrary, those who saw it said it seemed almost a youthful face, and one that bore a look of beatific peace.

Why Jimmie had been on the ladder in the first place no one knew. Strangely, the autopsy that followed found no injuries consistent with a fall: no broken bones, no bumps or bruises anywhere. It was, some said, as if a band of angels had been there to catch him as he fell and place him gently on the floor beside the tree.

Strange also was the matter of the light bulb wedged in Jimmie's trouser pocket. Amazingly, it too was unbroken in the fall. Some thought that Jimmie Bright had meant to use it to replace the bulb that lit the crystal star above the tree.

But when the guard who came upon the body that night looked up at the star, he saw it shone now with an even greater brilliance than it ever had before.

*T*he job had first belonged to Julio. Quite short and very muscular, Julio had been employed for two years in the shipping section of the store. Shipping was divided into two parts—the large high-ceilinged parcel room; and adjacent to it, through a set of massive swinging doors, the cargo platform and the open loading area that faced the street. Mostly, he worked outside trundling handcarts and flat rolling dollies, lifting packages, and generally joining the other men in filling or emptying the trucks that came and went continually throughout the day. Because of his great strength, combined with his diminutive proportions, his fellow workers called him Mighty Mouse, after the cartoon character.

One evening a week before Christmas, Julio approached his supervisor, Mr. Krupp. The man was seated at a battered wooden desk inside the parcel room, bludgeoning a stack of papers with a rubber stamp. He grunted an acknowledgment as Julio approached, but went on stamping forms without a pause.

Julio coughed several times, and between blows he announced apologetically to Mr. Krupp that he was leaving Shipping. He explained that he had been offered a position as a bellman in a deluxe hotel. He added hastily that although working on the loading docks had been the greatest experience of his life, he had been told a job as hotel bellman was the second greatest.

It was then Julio mentioned a cousin who could take his place. The cousin's name was Angel, and he was three years younger than Julio himself. Julio stressed, however, that Angel was a conscientious worker, hunching his powerful shoulders and flexing his biceps and deltoids so as to punctuate the affirmation of his cousin's worth.

The stamping ended, Mr. Krupp leaned back in his swivel chair and squinted narrowly at Julio. The supervisor was a stolid, humorless man with a totally bald head, pointed eyebrows, and a thin mouth that turned downward at the ends, which made him look like a dyspeptic mandarin. He was distrustful of all the men who worked for him, and those of Hispanic heritage he distrusted the most.

"Is he strong?" asked Mr. Krupp.

"Sí. Strong, yes," Julio said, flexing his arms again.

"Tell him to be here in the morning seven-thirty sharp," said Mr. Krupp. "This is our busy time."

So the next morning, at exactly seven-thirty, Julio's cousin Angel presented himself with great humility at the desk of Mr. Krupp.

While Julio had the physique of a bantam wrestler, Angel was thin and slight of build. Unlike his more swarthy cousin also, Angel had pale skin and limpid blue eyes that gave him the appearance of a youthful saint.

"You're him?" Mr. Krupp asked, rising, until he stood fully a head taller than Angel. "Julio said you were strong. Are you?"

Angel nodded.

"Ever done this kind of work before?"

Angel shook his head.

"What's the matter? Can't you talk?" Mr. Krupp looked visibly annoyed.

Again, Angel shook his head. He raised one hand and pointed to an ear, then to his open mouth, from which no sound came forth.

"What are you—a deaf-mute?"

Angel nodded, lowering his eyes in shame.

Mr. Krupp stared at the young man. Of the several things that Julio had said about his cousin this was not one of them. In fact, Angel had the capacity for speech. But a childhood illness had left him deaf in both ears, and for that reason he did not attempt to speak. Still, by going to a special school he had learned to read lips and to communicate in signs. In the rear pocket of his trousers he also carried a small pad and a pencil, so as to write messages when all other methods of expression failed.

"Okay," said Mr. Krupp at last. "Right now, I've got two trucks waiting at the docks outside. Start loading."

Angel nodded vigorously. He was about to give the man a grateful smile, but the supervisor had already dismissed him with a wave, and was walking off across the parcel room.

Being of a conscientious nature, and with great eagerness to please his new employer, Angel went about his labors in the loading area with all his heart. But in truth, he was not strong. As a result he toiled even harder than the other men, often arriving before dawn and remaining long into the night. When he returned to the apartment he shared with his mother and two younger sisters, he seldom had the strength or will to eat his supper before falling into an exhausted sleep.

Yet it was not the long hours Angel worked, nor the physical demands, that made the job most difficult. What was particularly painful was the incessant teasing he was forced to bear. Because of his unfortunate condition, some of Angel's fellow workers referred to him as the Speechless Spic or Silent Sam. Even his real name, Angel, became the object of their cruel jokes. Although they knew the correct pronunciation of the name was "Ahn-hel," many found malicious fun in addressing him as Angel Face, or with their fingers making halos in the air above their heads as he passed by.

Added to all this were the conditions under which the young man worked. Because he had assumed his cousin's job, Angel was required to be outside in the open loading area, rather than in the more protected parcel room. From Angel's first day on the job, the temperature had been extremely cold, so that by night his hands and face were raw and painful to the touch.

But the day of Christmas Eve was worse than all the others had been. The reason was the wind. It had begun before dawn, so that as Angel walked from the bus stop to the store, its fitful gusts were lifting bits of dirt and litter from the streets and flinging them into the air. By afternoon, it had increased to such intensity that its sharp icy fingers clawed into every open space; particularly, Angel thought, the loading area of the department store.

By fortunate coincidence, it happened that that morning, before Angel left for work, his mother had presented to him as an early Christmas gift a beautiful white scarf of thickest wool that she had knitted for her son. Throughout the day as Angel worked he kept the scarf pulled up inside the collar of his jacket, making certain that he wrapped it twice around his neck for warmth.

It was nearly nine o'clock that evening when he rolled an empty package dolly through the swinging doors into the parcel room and placed it to one side. Since it was Christmas Eve, the other men had long since gone. Only Mr. Krupp remained, seated at his desk, swearing angrily into the telephone. On the wall beyond him was the time clock used by the employees in Shipping. Angel headed to it. He had just taken the card with his name on it from the rack, and was about to insert it in the clock, when he saw Mr. Krupp slam down the phone and swear again.

He also saw the supervisor stand, hands held against his shining pate. "Hey, you. Angel. Do you want to stay tonight and make some overtime?"

Angel didn't. Tonight, on Christmas Eve, he wanted most to be at home with his mother and his sisters. But he knew how much all of them could use the extra money that the overtime would mean. And what would Mr. Krupp's reaction be if Angel answered no?

So Angel nodded. Yes, he indicated to the supervisor. He would stay.

"Good," said Mr. Krupp. "The problem is I got a truck that's broke down somewhere on the road. It won't get here for a coupla hours. And we can't close up till it does. You understand? *Comprende*, huh?"

The young man nodded.

Mr. Krupp reached back and took his jacket from a hook behind his chair. "I'm going to get some dinner. You stay here in case the truck comes."

Once more, Angel nodded to the man.

"Just don't do anything. And don't—repeat, do *not*—let anybody in the parcel room. A night like this, we get enough dirt blown in from the street. We don't need bums besides."

The supervisor turned, and slapped his open hand against the gray brick wall on which three words were painted, each in bold black letters almost a foot high.

AUTHORIZED PERSONS ONLY

warned the words along the wall.

"Maybe you can't speak or hear," said Mr. Krupp, "but you can read. 'Authorized Persons Only,' " he repeated, slapping each word one by one.

"That means no bums, no down-and-outs, no homeless in the parcel room. No*body*. Got it?"

Angel nodded yes, he understood.

Mr. Krupp thrust his arms into his jacket, pulled a wool cap from the pocket, and strode off in the direction of the swinging doors.

When Angel was certain that the boss was gone, he took a long deep breath. For an hour, probably longer, he alone would be the overseer of the Shipping section of the great department store. The responsibility weighed down on him with daunting suddenness. He wished he had a newspaper or magazine to read to pass the time, but there was none. Studying the vastness of the parcel room itself, he felt a chill that was made greater by the stark gray walks and the stone floor, fit-fully illuminated by the blue-white light of the fluorescent fixtures high above. He was glad that he still wore his jacket and the wool scarf, and he pulled up the scarf once again for warmth.

Now Angel began to walk. The walking seemed a way of focusing his mind. He walked along a narrow aisle, looking at the rows of boxes piled high on either side. If he saw a stack whose boxes were not evenly aligned, he straightened them. Starting up another aisle, Angel noticed on the floor some small white bits of package stuffing; they could be a hazard underfoot, he knew. So he bent and picked up every piece he saw and placed them in the refuse bin.

He was just emerging from around a row of boxes near the swinging doors when something made him stop. At first, he wasn't certain why. Then Angel realized the doors were moving slightly back and forth, as if they had been opened recently. He stood and watched until the motion finally stopped. It was the wind, he told himself; a gust had caused the doors to waver on their own. Even so, the thought that someone might have slipped into the parcel room unnerved him, and Angel wished that he were not alone.

But what if someone *had* sneaked inside from the street? What could Angel do? His deafness might prevent his knowing they were there until it was too late. He couldn't use the telephone to call for help. The wind, the young man told himself again. It had to be the wind.

With that he turned into another aisle—and abruptly stopped. Ahead, not more than twenty feet away, he saw a man. The man was turned away from him, addressing someone out of Angel's sight.

Lying on the floor within his reach, Angel observed, was a piece of jagged wood that had been splintered from a packing crate. He knelt, picked it up, and stood again. Now holding the piece of wood out before him like a baseball bat, he moved with slow, deliberate resolve in the direction of the man.

He had only gone a few steps when the man turned and stared at him.

Angel stared as well. The man was bearded, and though poor and weary with exhaustion, there was no malice in his eyes. To Angel's great surprise, in fact, they shone with gentleness and trust. But what most surprised Angel was that his own eyes moved now to the person the man had been addressing. It was a young woman. Seated on a wooden box, she, too, was dressed in a thin coat, and now and then she shivered from the cold. Yet looking at her, Angel saw her face was beautiful; her hair was long and lustrously soft, her eyes deep-set. As she gazed up at Angel now, there was a sense of peace about her, a serenity that seemed to fill the room itself. Angel noticed, too, that she was very pregnant.

Angel lay the piece of wood aside.

"Good evening," the man said to him. "I'm sorry if we—"

Angel shook his head. He pointed to an ear and then his mouth.

"I'm sorry," said the man. "Can you read lips?"

Angel nodded; yes, he could.

"Then help us. Please. We need a place to rest, my wife and I. If you will let us stay here just for—"

But already Angel had begun to shake his head. Sympathetic though he was, the orders given to him by the supervisor were inviolable. Absolutely *no one* was permitted in the parcel room. He walked over to the wall and pointed to the words themselves. As Mr. Krupp had done, he placed an open hand against the words. Then with a single pointed finger, Angel tapped each word in turn.

AUTHORIZED—the finger tapped, then lifted—moving next to PERSONS—lifting, moving on to ONLY for a final tap. AUTHORIZED (tap), PERSONS (tap), ONLY (tap)—Angel repeated the command.

"I understand," the man assured him. "But we're strangers in the city, and we've walked all day. My wife is very tired. For her sake, especially, we need a place to rest."

Just then the woman uttered a small cry.

The husband sat down on the box beside her. "Soon?" he asked, and took her hand.

"Yes. Very soon," she said.

The infant was a boy, healthy and robust. Before his birth, however, Angel took the rolling package dolly from the place where he had parked it, and he helped the father fashion it into a bed. To soften its flat surface, Angel gathered all the quilted packing blankets he could find in the supply closet and spread them out across the dolly, folding several into makeshift pillows for the mother's head. Others were drawn up around the mother and the child to protect them from the coldness of the room.

Now lying in his mother's arms the child slept. On a box beside them both, the father sat and held her hand in his. At a respectful distance from the new young family, Angel stood and gazed in silent wonder at them all. Why God had chosen this cold night and these inhospitable surroundings to bring a child into the world, Angel couldn't understand. Even in the corner of the room where they had placed the dolly bed, dark shadows from the rows of parcels fell across the scene. Yet as he studied the tableau of the parents and the child, Angel felt a spirit that infused the room with warmth and light.

The child stirred. At once, the mother drew up a corner of the packing quilt around him, while she rocked him in her arms. Angel wished he had another quilt to give them both. But he had taken all the unused ones that he could find.

Then Angel thought about the white wool scarf his mother had given him that morning as a gift. He removed it from beneath the collar of his jacket, held it in his hands, and looked at it. The wool was very soft and still warm from where it had been against his skin. It saddened him to part with it. But he was sure that when he explained the reason to his mother she would understand.

Angel stepped forward. With the scarf extended, he indicated to the mother that she use it for a covering to wrap the child in.

The young woman smiled up at Angel. "Thank you. You are very kind," she said. She took the scarf, and cradling the infant, wrapped him gently in the folds of the wool.

Angel stepped away again. He was embarrassed at the inadequacy of the gift, but there was nothing more that he could offer.

Food. He could bring food. The man and woman must be very hungry after their day of wandering the streets. There was a coffee shop a block from the department store. He could run to it, order something from the take-out section, and be back in very little time.

The infant suddenly awoke and gave a lusty cry. At once both parents sought to comfort him. As they began to, Angel headed toward the swinging doors.

Running with the wind against him, he reached the coffee shop at last, and went inside. He paused briefly, to regain his breath, then hurried to the counter where the take-out items were dispensed. He saw a soiled menu in a metal stand beside the countertop and opened it. When the counterman approached him, Angel pointed to the Special of the Day—a tuna roll with a toasted bun. Angel raised a pair of fingers, indicating to the counterman it was a double order. Pointing to the menu card again, he requested two containers of hot coffee, with some cream and sugar packets added on the side. The counterman began to place the order in a paper bag, and as Angel watched, awareness of his own considerable hunger grew. He tapped the counter sharply, then gestured to the items in the bag, suggesting he would like another tuna roll and a coffee for himself. When they were finally placed among them, Angel nodded to the counterman, grabbed up the paper bag, and went to the cashier.

The bill for what he'd purchased came to ten dollars and some change. Angel dug into his pocket—and remembered with a sinking feeling he'd loaned most of the money he had had that morning to his younger sister for her school lunch. Counting out the coins in his open hand, he found they totaled one dollar and twenty-seven cents. It was just enough to buy a token for his bus ride home that night.

Angel added up the coins for a second time. As he did, the line behind him grew impatient. So did the cashier. Angel, in turn, peered at the numbers on the register, then at the bag of food he still gripped in one hand.

Slowly, Angel pushed the bag aside. He nodded sheepishly at the cashier—then darted empty-handed from the coffee shop.

Outside on the street once more, he pressed against a building and endeavored to sort out the confusion in his mind. Gone were any thoughts of Mr. Krupp or the truck they were awaiting at the loading docks. All that mattered was to find food for the young couple; nothing else was of concern. He thought of stopping people on the street and asking, begging, them for money. But the wind had long ago discouraged most from venturing outside, and those few hurried past without a glance.

Looking farther down the street, he saw a lighted canopy. It marked the entrance of a fashionable restaurant. Angel pulled up the collar of his jacket as far as it would go and headed for the restaurant at a run. Yet on reaching it, he hesitated and retreated a short distance, deciding what his plan of action ought to be. He watched as well-dressed men and women came and went through the elaborately carved wooden doors. As poorly dressed as he was, he couldn't simply enter in their company and ask the restaurant manager to give him food.

Nearby was a narrow alley bordering the building that the restaurant occupied. Angel guessed that somewhere along it was a door that led directly to the kitchen. It was worth a try. He went down the alley, and as he suspected, found an unmarked metal door. He knocked against the metal, and when there was no answer, hit it with his fist.

To his surprise, the door was opened in an instant. Filling the entire doorway was an enormous jowly man in a white apron and chef's hat.

"If you're the new dishwasher, you're late," the chef said.

Angel shook his head. Again, he pointed to his ear and then his mouth. He reached into his back pocket for his pad and pencil and quickly wrote: "Please, sir, I need food for—"

"Beat it, dummy," said the chef. He gave Angel a shove into the alleyway and slammed the door.

Angel turned away. It was no use. He'd failed in his hope of finding food. There was no time to go on seeking it, and he had little money, anyway, to buy it if he did. All he could do was to go back to the parcel room, apologize to the young couple, and explain to them that he had tried.

The quickest route back to the department store, he thought, was to continue down the alley to the street beyond. So he ran in that direction, turned, and found himself instead within an open cul-de-sac.

And he was not alone. Confronting Angel were a half dozen homeless men and women ringed around a blazing oil drum. A few held plastic cups. Others passed a loaf of bread among them, each tearing off a piece to eat.

A woman near the fire beckoned to Angel.

A man dressed in a parka with the hood pulled up stepped toward him. "Have some food. There's soup," the man informed him. "Also bread."

He pointed to the flaming drum. Across the top of

it a metal grating had been placed. A large pot rested on the grate; from it great clouds of vapor rose into the air.

"You look like you could use some soup," the hooded figure said. He found an empty cup and moved to fill it with a ladle that was resting in the pot.

"What's your name?" the figure asked him, as the cup was filled.

Angel raised a hand. He was about to gesture to his ear when the woman who had beckoned to him raised her hands, made several quick configurations with them, and in sign language asked Angel if he could communicate in kind.

Delighted, Angel answered quickly, with his own hands, that, indeed, he could.

What is your name? her hands asked.

Angel told her.

"His name is Angel," said the woman to the others.

But already Angel's hands were moving eagerly before him, saying more. And as his fingers formed the signs, the woman translated his words, speaking them aloud to all those gathered there around the fire.

Thus, Angel told of what he had been witness to that night. Hands flying in the air, he told of the young man and woman who had sought shelter in the parcel room of the department store. He told, then, of the birth; how small, yet perfect, seemed the child; how serene and beautiful the mother was; and how the father showed such tender caring for them both. Angel told also of the joy he himself knew and the peace that overcame him as he gazed upon the infant sleeping in his mother's arms.

And as he told these things in signs, and the woman

spoke them to the crowd, the others listened, saying nothing, so in awe were they of what they heard.

Carrying two plastic cups, Angel pushed aside the swinging doors into the parcel room, and stopped. Mr. Krupp had not returned, nor had the long-awaited truck arrived at the loading docks. The mother continued to recline, half lying on her bed of quilts. The child slept, still wrapped in Angel's scarf. Beside them, on a wooden box, the father remained seated, speaking in reassuring whispers to his wife.

Angel came to them at once and offered them the cups. Each contained the soup the homeless men and women had provided him.

The father rose and took the cups from Angel's hands. "Thank you," he said. "You're very kind."

Angel reached into his pocket and also gave the man the portion of the loaf of bread he had received.

The man put down the soup and took the bread. "Let me repay you," the man said. "I have a little money still."

But Angel shook his head. While the couple ate, he went back to the supervisor's desk. He had decided that if Mr. Krupp should suddenly appear and find the couple and the child here, he would be fired on the spot. He didn't care. In fact, he was more certain now than ever that he'd been right to let the family stay. But for how long would they remain?

As if in answer to his thoughts, a short time later the man approached Angel at the desk. "My wife and I—we cannot be more grateful to you for the food and shelter you have given us," the man said. "But now she and our child should be in a hospital where they can have proper care. If I may, I'd like to call the hospital and ask that they be taken there tonight."

Angel agreed. As the man began to place the call, Angel indicated to him that he would stand beside the swinging doors, awaiting the arrival of the ambulance.

Angel had just reached the doors when they began to open and another man appeared. It was the homeless figure in the hood and parka who had befriended him, had called him to the blazing fire, and who had offered him the food.

"Where is the child?" the man asked him.

Startled and unsure what he should answer, Angel gestured toward the room.

The man nodded, turned, and called back through the open doors. "Come, follow me."

Suddenly, behind the man more came—the other homeless men and women to whom Angel had told the story of the birth. But what amazed him was that they were followed by still others; strangers Angel had never seen before, but moving in a slow and steady line behind the hooded man.

As he drew near the dolly where the mother and the child lay, the man pushed back his hood. Then pausing, he knelt down and bowed his head. The silent moments passed. At last, the man rose and with his head still bowed, moved toward the doors once more, returning to the night. Now, all those who came after him did just as he had, each in turn. Those wearing hats or caps removed them. In the presence of the mother and the child, each one knelt, head bowed in reverence, before arising, finally, and moving on.

The doors had hardly closed behind the last of them when Angel saw the pulsing red light of the ambulance as it came down the street. It stopped and backed into a loading bay.

Less than five minutes after the arrival of the ambulance, the vehicle pulled out onto the street again. Aboard it were the mother, father, and the child. Angel stood on the cargo platform and watched until it disappeared from view.

Alone, he turned and walked slowly back into the parcel room. He gathered up the packing quilts that were still lying on the dolly. Folding each quilt carefully, he carried them to the supply closet and returned them to the shelves. Next, he rolled the dolly back to its accustomed place beside the wall. The empty cups that had contained the soup he discarded in the refuse bin. Looking out across the room at last, it appeared exactly as it was when Mr. Krupp had left. The gray brick walls, the flickering fluorescent lights above, the rows of boxes reaching almost to the ceiling—none gave witness to the strange and wonderful events that had occurred within the room that night.

Then two things happened simultaneously: Mr. Krupp strode into the parcel room, and the telephone began to ring. The supervisor went directly to his desk and took the phone. He listened, scowling. He swore very loudly. Then he slammed the phone down on the desk.

"That was the driver of our truck," the supervisor said. "It won't be here tonight. Go home."

Angel gave a noncommittal nod. He went to the rack that held the time cards, removed his and placed it in the clock. He noticed the late hour; soon it would be Christmas Day. Angel thought of taking out his little pad and writing "Merry Christmas, Mr. Krupp." But the man was busy at his desk, preparing papers for the day after tomorrow, when the work would start again. Angel shrugged and headed off.

He made his way across the parcel room and pushed out through the swinging doors. As he reached the street, he was surprised to find the wind had stopped and the winter night was not as chill. He looked up and discovered that the sky that arched above the building tops displayed a panoply of stars.

Walking toward the bus stop, Angel thought of the young couple, and of the child born to them tonight inside the parcel room. Then he remembered the admonition on the wall above the supervisor's desk.

AUTHORIZED PERSONS ONLY

Angel admitted to himself that even now he wasn't sure of the meaning of the word *authorized*. His first day on the job, he'd looked up the definition in the small pocket dictionary he carried in order to improve his language skills. "Authorized," the dictionary said; "established by authority"; "Authority—power, influence . . ."

The young man and woman who had found refuge in the parcel room had had no power, no influence, no authority. Yet many, upon hearing of their newborn son, had come to look upon the child and to honor him. So, too, centuries ago, others had paid homage to a child at the time of His Nativity, because they saw in Him the promise of a better world than the one they knew.

Many had brought gifts to the manger of that child then. Tonight, the only gift this child had received was Angel's white wool scarf. Still, the young mother had accepted it with gratitude, and wrapped the infant in the softness of its folds. As the mother and the child had been placed aboard the ambulance, Angel had been pleased to see the scarf was still around him, warming and protecting him as he lay sleeping in her arms.

By chance, the place where Angel hoped to find a bus was opposite a church. Now as he stood waiting at the curb, he looked up at the clock in the church tower and discovered it was twelve o'clock—the start of Christmas Day. Thinking back to when he was a child, Angel recalled a tale of a person who was good of heart to whom a miracle had happened at the stroke of midnight Christmas Day.

"Excuse me, sir."

The speaker was a beggar. He had stepped forward from a darkened doorway with his hand outstretched.

"Excuse me," said the beggar to Angel. "But it's Christmas. Would you have some coins you could spare a poor man on this holy day?"

Angel reached into his pocket, and his fingers found the dollar and twenty-seven cents he had been saving for the bus ride home. He paused, then drew the coins out and gave them to the man.

The beggar took the coins, bowed his head, and grasped hold of Angel's hands.

"God bless you, sir," the beggar said. "And Merry Christmas."

"Merry Christmas," said Angel.

you as a friend, and not merely as a customer. And
know you and admire you for the romantic ways in which

MR. CAVANAUGH'S CHRISTMAS

ilent Night."

I hear the music of the Christmas carol drifting
faintly from some distant place within the store. The
source is probably a radio belonging to a guard or a
member of the cleaning staff as they go about their evening chores. Otherwise, the night is indeed silent, except
for the fitful scratching of my pen against the pad on
which I write these words.

This is the last of my tales of the Christmas Store.
Like the others I have given it a title, which suggests that
like them it has a definite beginning and an end. Such is
not the case. I will acknowledge that the true beginning
of this story, my story, is uncertain. As for its conclusion, I am reluctant to predict. Stories, too, are written
to be read by many people. Again, in my own case, that
is not my expectation or my wish.

Why then do I begin at all, if what I write is for my eyes alone? The truth is that I write to reaffirm my being; and in this account to make a record of my life, such as it is. I admit it: I take pleasure in certain facts about myself of which I am most proud. I am proud of my name—Thomas J. Cavanaugh. I am proud also of my association with the Gentlemen's Apparel section of the store, in which I worked for many years. The very sight of me, I'm told, encouraged other men, who had achieved a certain station in their lives, to purchase fine suits similar to mine.

Although I left my job in Gentlemen's Apparel several years ago, I was surprised and pleased to find myself reactivated temporarily for the holidays. Therefore, beginning the day after Thanksgiving until the night of Christmas Eve, I roam about the store assisting and advising customers, and if needed, aiding in a sale here and there.

Yet if what I witness for myself, or have related to me, forms the basis of my stories, why then am I hesitant to write my own? Would it be wiser at this point to discard the several pages I have filled and say no more? I know it would.

Still, should I continue with this curious account, it will allow me to articulate the circumstances of my past and present situation, and in so doing to explain and justify my life. . . .

It was a Friday evening early in December—I vividly recall the night because it snowed. It began at dusk; occasional small flakes that floated earthward from the low dun-colored clouds. So rapidly did they intensify, however, that by the time the closing bells were sounded in the store, the streets and buildings of the city had been overspread with a duvet of deepest white. Members of the store's maintenance department were dispatched to clear the sidewalks, but the broad blades of their shovels were no match for the blizzardlike conditions that soon held the city in its grip. While guards from store security stood by the doors exhorting laggard customers to leave, I too stood looking at the lines of weary, package-laden shoppers as they filed out into the fearsome night. Watching them was a reminder of how fortunate I was to be enjoying the warmth and comfort of the store.

When the last customers had made their exit, and the guards had locked the doors, I turned and started toward the bank of elevators that would take me to the Stationery section several floors above. It was there that I spent several hours every evening writing down my observations of the day. Boarding the first car, I had a change of mind, and instead pressed the button for the floor on which television sets were sold.

As I arrived, I saw the section manager. We greeted one another, and I asked him if I might view one of the many sets that stood about the floor. The man had no objection, but since he was also leaving for the night, he asked only that I switch it off when I was done. I promised that I would. We wished each other a good night.

As it happened, I switched on not one set but three, each carrying live bulletins about the storm. I watched, fascinated, for as long as the reports continued, thinking still how pleasant my surroundings were when contrasted with the harsh, inclement weather that existed outside of the department store itself. Finally, I turned off the three sets and resumed my journey up to Stationery.

From the supply cabinet in the rear hall, I removed the leatherbound portfolio from its shelf and continued to the sales floor. Usually, I had a period of solitude in which to write before the cleaning staff appeared. But not tonight. As I sat down at the small writing desk I used, I heard the trundling of cleaning apparatus and the voices of men and women as they approached this corner of the floor. Leading the way was Wendell, the chief of the crew, with his pomaded hair, emptying wastebaskets left and right. Behind him came his brother Damien, pushing a rolling bin into which Wendell's wastebaskets were dumped. In their wake followed four women in gray uniforms, three of whom pulled vacuum cleaners as they moved along the aisles. The fourth woman, who was younger than the rest, carried a large dust rag, which she applied enthusiastically to shelves and tabletops.

Despite their presence on the floor, I decided I would make the best of it. I opened the portfolio and had written several sentences—when I became aware that I was being watched. I glanced up, and was startled to discover that the woman with the dust rag was regarding me with intense curiosity. I nodded a brief greeting, principally to let her know that I was conscious of her stare. She smiled quickly, turned to a display shelf full of notecards, and went on about her work.

As she did, I took the opportunity to study her as well. She was in her thirties, tall but well proportioned, with a long, handsome face and almond eyes. But what drew my particular attention was her red hair, which tumbled down around her shoulders to her back. In her stride and movements, there was a healthy energy, a verve that showed her zest for life.

I returned once more to my writing, and had filled a page, before I realized that she was dusting ever closer to my desk. Soon, her dust rag flew across the surface of a teakwood chest directly opposite me on which paperweights were spread. I set aside my pen, and looked at her as she continued with her work.

Suddenly, her dust rag brushed a paperweight and knocked it to the floor. "Oh, dear," she cried. She knelt, retrieved the object, and replaced it on the chest. She stood up, and apologized at once. "Excuse me, sir. If you're the manager of Stationery, I'm so sorry. It won't happen again."

"I'm not the manager," I told her.

"A salesman then?"

"No."

"I thought you might be one or the other. Working overtime and all. This is my first night on the job."

"I see."

"I hardly got here as it was. It's snowing out to beat the band."

"I gather so from what the television showed. I haven't been outside."

"Well, if you're thinking to stay late, you should think otherwise. The traffic's terrible." She smiled quickly, as she had before.

"Thank you for telling me," I said. "But I don't live far away."

"You're luckier than I am then. I'm clear across town." She came forward to the desk and offered me her hand. "Oh, let me introduce myself—I'm Annie Calloway."

I rose and took it. "How do you do? I'm Mr. Cavanaugh."

Our hands parted, but I sensed that she was studying my features with the same quizzical expression I had noticed earlier.

At last, she stepped back from the desk. "Well—glad to be of your acquaintance, Mr. Cavanaugh. And get home safe."

"I'm sure I will. Thank you."

She bestowed her smile on me one last time before taking up her dust rag and directing it along a row of nearby shelves.

Throughout the next day I thought about our meeting. On the one hand, our encounter, although brief, had been an interruption in my work. But I had also found the woman's openness engaging. What's more, there was an ingenuous and earthy quality about her that added to her charm. I will confess, in fact, that as the day wore on I looked forward once again to chatting with her as I had the night before.

To my surprise, however, such was not to be the case. The second night, and for the several nights that followed, she appeared reluctant to approach me. When she did, she gave me no more than her quick smile, and continued dusting everything she faced without a pause.

Then, late one evening, well after the cleaning staff had come and gone, and I myself was ready to retire for the night, I was surprised to look up and discover her opposite me, dressed in a plain coat and holding a cup and saucer in her hand.

"Wendell scolded me," she said. "I'm sorry, sir."

"I beg your pardon?"

"The head cleaner, Wendell, scolded me for bothering you the night of the big snow. Did you get home all right?"

"Uh—yes, I did."

"I'm glad. It took me hours. Anyway, I made some tea for you tonight before I left. Seeing how you're working late again." She placed the cup of tea before me on the desk.

"Thank you very much." I sipped the tea, and found it strong but good.

"There's generally a kettle going in the ladies' changing room. I didn't think to bring you sugar, though. I can go back."

"No. This is fine. It's very good."

"Good night then, Mr. Cavanaugh."

"Good night."

In the week that followed she brought me tea each night before she left the store. Always, we would chat for several minutes. In our brief conversations, I discovered that she was a recent widow, having lost her husband well before his time. It was apparently a very loving marriage, but there were no children, she admitted, much to her regret. She had grown up in the country, she said, and had moved to the city after she and Mr. Calloway were married. She remembered how as newlyweds they had come here to the department store to shop, but also to admire all the beautiful objects that they planned to buy someday.

And on those evenings, after Mrs. Calloway had gone, I would reflect upon our visit and how pleasant it had been. Being friendly and gregarious and genuinely good, she'd taken it upon herself each night to brew the tea and bring a cup to me before she headed home. True, she was a widow without children; there was no other person in her life, it seemed, for whom to do small kindnesses as she had done for me.

Even so, the more I pondered it, the more her simple thoughtfulness affected me. And as it did, an unfamiliar feeling overcame me, a sensation I had never known before. But of one thing I was certain. In the company of Annie Calloway, I was a very happy man.

Good evening, Mr. Cavanaugh."

"Good evening, Mrs. Calloway."

She stood before me as she always did, dressed in her coat, a cup and saucer in her hand.

This time her eyes teased me with their playfulness. "I brought you a surprise," she said. "Can you guess what it is?"

I shook my head.

"Go on. Try."

"I give up. What's your surprise?"

"Today I baked some cookies to go with your tea." She set the cup and saucer on the desk, then reached into her purse. From it she withdrew a little box, and placed it on the desk beside the tea. "There's pinwheels, and molasses crisps, and ginger men. And shortbread, too."

"I'm sure I'll like them all. Please, have some with me."

"Well—you might want to bring some home."

"No. I don't have anyone to share them with." I saw her take note of my unplanned admission.

"Please—" I said again, and moved the box in her direction, opening it as I did.

She took a ginger man, sat down on a stool near the desk, and unbuttoned her coat. At the same time, I pulled out a molasses crisp and sampled it. "Delicious—very good," I said.

My pleasure obviously pleased her, too. "I've always loved to bake at Christmas—cookies, fruitcakes, pies. My husband's favorite was mincemeat."

"Did you know," I said, "that in the Middle Ages people were encouraged to eat twelve mincemeat pies at Christmas, so as to have twelve months of good fortune in the year ahead?"

"One is quite enough for me. I'd burst if I ate twelve." She laughed, and held the ginger man at bay as if it were a pie. "What other Christmas customs do you know?"

"Well, what we call Christmas may have started as an ancient Roman festival. Two festivals, in fact. The feast of Saturnalia, in memory of old King Saturn, and the feast of Kalends, when people decorated homes with lights and greens."

"Good heavens. Where did you learn all that?"

"From books."

"And what about the Christmas stocking? When I was a little girl I loved seeing all the gifts my stocking had."

I smiled, warming to my subject now. "The tradition probably began in France in the Middle Ages, when treats were wrapped in stockings to be given to the children of the poor."

She seemed delighted with my expertise. "I'll think of that the next time I go past the giant stocking down the street. You know the one I mean."

I hesitated. "No—I'm not sure that I do."

She looked surprised. "Of course you do! It's several stories tall. It's hanging from the building roof a block from here. What direction do you go when you go home?"

I felt a sudden dryness in my mouth and drank some tea. "Well—I don't think of the direction, really."

Disbelief was written on her face. "How can a man who knows so much from books not know how he gets home?"

I waved vaguely to my right. "It's probably that way."

"Then you go right by it!" Her astonishment gave way to laughter once again. "You carry so much knowledge in your head, you never think of looking up to see what's over it!"

Relieved, I joined in the laughter, too. "I guess you're right. Next time, I'll be sure to notice it." I drank down the remainder of the tea.

"If you're leaving soon, I'll wait and we can walk together. I go that way myself."

"No, no," I answered quickly. "I still have some loose ends to tidy up. You go ahead."

Mrs. Calloway regarded me. Then, acquiescing, she rose and rebuttoned her coat.

"But thank you again for the cookies and the tea," I added pleasantly.

"You're welcome."

I expected her to turn and go. Instead, she peered at me with the same quizzical expression I remembered from the night we met.

"I don't know if I should tell you this," she said, with some uncertainty. "But my first night on the job—the first time I saw you sitting here—you reminded me of someone."

"Oh?"

"Somebody from long ago. That's why I stared."

"I see."

She looked embarrassed, but amused at the same time. "Since then I've been trying to remember when it was. Then last night it came to me. I told you how my husband and I used to visit this department store. He also took a special pride in how he dressed. So every time, we'd stop in Gentlemen's Apparel to admire all the fine men's clothes. Well, near the entrance to the section was this handsome man. He wore a dark blue suit like you do, and he had the same black hair, and eyes like yours. Even the white handkerchief he wore in his breast pocket was the same as what you're wearing now. Except the man—the figure was a mannequin."

Embarrassment now fully overcame her, and she lowered her eyes. "That's an awful thing to say to anyone—that they remind you of a mannequin." She raised her eyes again. "Truth is, you're better-looking than that mannequin—and lots more lively, too."

She picked up the cup and saucer. "Look how late it is. I should be going. But I'm so glad you liked the cookies. If you want, I'll make some more tomorrow night."

I nodded, but said nothing.

In a short time Mrs. Calloway was gone.

What I am about to write is done so beneath the single bare bulb that illuminates the basement storage room of the department store that houses mannequins. This I will say at once: I have no intention of continuing my evening visits to the Stationery section of the store, since I do not wish to run the risk of ever seeing Mrs. Calloway again. She will believe, of course, that I was deeply hurt by her remark suggesting I resembled a store mannequin. But what I feel most is shame. For unwittingly, that kind and cheerful woman has exposed the truth of who—or, rather, what—I am.

Mannequin. The word is French, from the Dutch, meaning literally "little man." I find the definition almost as demeaning as the word *dummy* to denote a figure modeled in the likeness of a human being for the display of clothes.

I have learned from store employees that I arrived here some years ago with a shipment of a dozen adult mannequins. After being dressed in a dark blue pinstriped suit, I was placed on a low pedestal near the entranceway of Gentleman's Apparel. Five years ago, however, after I was knocked to the floor by a rolling rack of suits, I was inspected and considered to be "out of date." Newer models were being manufactured now of special plastics and epoxy, instead of the pressed wood of which I had been made.

There was, I gather, a small farewell party given in honor of my removal from the floor. It took place on the day before Thanksgiving. After the store closed, the salesmen of Gentleman's Apparel stood around me with their glasses raised to celebrate my long career. I was then unceremoniously strapped onto a handcart and transported to this basement room where unused mannequins are stored.

What followed the next morning may be regarded as a miracle. I now consider it a cruel joke. At dawn, I "awakened" to discover I was staring at a brick wall, standing in a group of several dozen other male mannequins as unclothed as myself. Yet unlike them I was now a mortal man imbued with life; a marvelous assemblage of senses and of sensibilities—of eyes that saw, and limbs that moved, and best of all, a mind with the capacity for thought.

Feeling cold suddenly, I noticed in the dimness of the room a garment hanging on the wall. I later learned it was a smock worn by the store's window dressers when they decorated the displays. I put it on, and proceeding to move slowly, made a tour of the room. I reached the door at last, and finding it unlocked, I left at once. By some instinctive reasoning, I went directly to the Gentlemen's Apparel section, where I acquired articles of clothing—suit, shirt, necktie, socks, and shoes; and yes, a pocket handkerchief—in which I dressed myself.

Thus attired, I began my journey of discovery of the department store. Because it was Thanksgiving Day (the concept of the holiday did not have meaning for me at the time), there were no salesclerks or customers about. Guards must have been on duty, but I encountered none. The tiny cameras used by store security to monitor the halls and stairways might have caught my image. Yet my presence was unchallenged anywhere I went. And I went everywhere. From the basement to the top floor of the building, I investigated every corner I could find. In Clocks, I marveled at the sound that followed when the hour struck. In Furniture, I lay for many minutes in a lounging chair fingering the buttons that directed the footrest to move up and down. When afternoon arrived, I had my first experience with hunger. Since I was in the Bath Shop at the time, I bit into a bar of soap. I realized at once I still had much to learn about what human beings ate.

Still, it was that night as I walked on about the store that I had the most startling experience of my brief life. A man—a guard, as it turned out—was staring at a box within which people moved and talked. Watching from a distance, I learned, too, that when the people in the glowing box began to yawn as I was doing now, they lay down on an object called a bed and slept. That night I had my first sleep in a canopied four-poster in the Beds and Bedding section of the store.

I arose early the next morning and resumed my wanderings. Soon, salesclerks appeared and took their places. After them came customers pouring in among the aisles. And all the while I continued looking, listening, and learning everything I could about this marvelous new world into which I had been thrust. From hearing people speak, I gained the gift of language, and was able to converse. In the Food department, I observed the wonderful baked goods, and was delighted when a countergirl, thinking me a store employee, gave me a sweet roll and a cup of coffee to enjoy.

Nonetheless, when evening came again, I sensed that I should not return to Bedding. My birthplace, so to speak, had been the basement storage room, and it was there I knew that I should make my home. After the store closed I went to Camp Equipment, where I stealthily removed a sleeping bag and folding cot. These I carried to the storage room. To prevent a night guard from discovering me while I slept, I hid the cot and sleeping bag behind a crowd of unclothed female mannequins. Besides protecting me from prying eyes, it encouraged the most wonderful of dreams.

A word about my name. It happened on the third night of my life. As I was readying myself for sleep, my bare right foot struck a corner of the cot. In doing so, a wooden splinter pierced my toe. I raised my foot to pluck the splinter out. But in looking at the sole of my foot, I was amazed to see the words stamped into it:

Designed and Manufactured by
THOMAS J. CAVANAUGH & SONS
Makers of Fine Mannequins

So it was he—Thomas Cavanaugh—from whose factory I came. It gave me comfort, I confess, to know who my creator was. I decided then that if I am the product of his handiwork, I should be deeply proud to bear his name.

As for my knowledge of the world beckoning beyond the walls of the department store, I learned of it in part from looking at the store's many television sets, the "glowing boxes" of my early days. But it was from books that my true understanding of that world came. My last stop before returning to the storage room at night would be the Books section of the store. I would take a book and in the quiet of the room consume its contents. I would return it first thing in the morning to the same shelf from which I'd taken it the night before.

I also learned from books a curious phenomenon that certain animals are subject to. It is a kind of long and dreamless sleep. Bears and other creatures hibernate for many months before they wake and stir. And so it is with me. Each year my active waking life, which begins the morning of Thanksgiving, ends again on Christmas night. As the holiday draws to a close, I feel a great weariness, a torpor, overtaking me. Returning to the storage room, I fold my cot and sleeping bag, and hide them in the dark recesses of the room. Then I undress and hide my clothes. At last, I take my place among the other standing mannequins. Staring at the wall, my eyelids droop. They close. And there I stand—a mannequin again—until the morning of the next Thanksgiving dawns.

Tonight it is the evening of December 23—a full week since I last saw Mrs. Calloway. Is it my cowardice that leads me to avoid her? Perhaps. But I believe that to encourage any further friendship with her, however innocent, would be unwise. By now, she will be concerned as to the reason for my absence. She may wonder if some accident or illness has befallen me. She may make inquiries among the others of the cleaning staff as to my whereabouts. They, of course, will be as perplexed as she. Still, as the nights stretch into weeks and months, and I do not appear, she will forget me more and more, of that I'm sure.

As for the daytime hours, I have continued on my rounds about the store. At first, I was afraid our paths might cross. But I concluded that the chances of it happening are slim. Because she works at night, she probably sleeps a good part of the morning. Two other factors predicate against our meeting: first, the crowds this season are particularly large; and they are moving constantly, myself among them. Nevertheless, I maintain a watchful eye. Should I see Mrs. Calloway, I would make every effort to avoid her.

Saddened though I am to say so, I believe that I will never see her again.

How wrong I was!

Today—December 24—it happened. The closing bell had sounded through the store, and customers were streaming toward the exit doors. I was in an aisle on the main floor when I heard her call my name.

I turned to see her staring at me with a look of stunned relief.

"Mr. Cavanaugh! It's you!"

"Ah—yes . . . Mrs. Calloway. How do you do?" I was as surprised as she.

"I was afraid— Are you all right?"

"A winter cold," I said, searching for a plausible excuse.

"But now you're better?"

"Yes."

"I'm *so* glad. I was afraid I wouldn't see you before Christmas. Will I see you up in Stationery later on?"

"No. Actually—I'm leaving soon."

"Oh?"

"Doctor's orders." I tapped my chest and gave a mild cough.

"Then what luck we ran into one another." She touched my hand, then reached into her pocket and drew out a small envelope. "I wrote this after the last time I saw you. I've been carrying it ever since."

She pressed the envelope into my hand. "I hope you can. I do." With that, she turned away and disappeared into the crowd.

I thrust the envelope into my own pocket, baffled as to what the note contained. Curiosity gave way to apprehension. I left the sales floor at once and sought refuge in a deserted hallway. There, I hastily retrieved the envelope. Examining it closely now, I saw my own name written in a flowing hand across the front. My fingers trembled as I opened it. Inside was a note. It read—

Dear Mr. Cavanaugh,

Last night when you were telling me about the Christmases of long ago, I got to thinking of this Christmas just a week or so away, and what your plans might be. Then I thought—Annie Calloway, you've got a nice apartment and you love to cook. Why don't you invite Mr. Cavanaugh to come to dinner Christmas Day?

No need to call. Is two o'clock okay?

Oh, do please come. It is my fondest Christmas wish.

Yours in the spirit of the holiday,
Annie Calloway

Her address followed at the bottom of the page. I read the note a second time. As I did, an image of her filled my mind—the bright eyes, the tumbling red hair, a woman full of earthy humor and of life. I saw her, too, tomorrow—Christmas Day—alone and waiting, hoping I would come to her and share the simple dinner she had made.

Well, why shouldn't I go? I asked myself. I could slip out through the door used by employees. Old Timothy, who guards the door on holidays, will let me pass. I'll make my way to Mrs. Calloway's, and spend several hours enjoying her dinner and her company. It will allow me ample time to return to the department store before I must prepare for my protracted slumber in the storage room.

I slipped the note into an inside pocket, left the hallway, and began to cross the floor. By now the store was empty of all customers, and most of the sales staff as well. As I walked past the large glass doors that led out to the street, I saw beyond them nothing but the darkness of the winter night. I paused, peering through the glass.

As I stood looking out into the darkness, doubts assailed me. Was it folly even to set foot outside the store? Out there in the night-enshrouded city that I looked upon, I knew that there was want and sadness, circumstances that would never touch me if I stayed within this brightly lighted world of the store. Within these walls, I dine on gourmet food whenever I desire it, and dress in clothes that are supreme examples of the tailor's art. For me this store is a true paradise. Dare I risk everything I have to leave it, even for the short time I had planned?

I resolved to go on to the storage room and reconsider my decision. I was about to turn away when something caught my eye. I turned back—and saw pressed against the outside surface of the glass door a child's hand. It was a girl of about six or seven. She wore a simple coat and cap. She stood, her hand spread flat against the door, and smiled up at me.

For a reason I cannot explain, I raised my hand, and opposite the spot where she had put her tiny palm, I placed my own. We stood for several moments—the child and myself—our two hands separated only by the hard, cold thinness of the glass.

It was then the answer came to me. If I am to touch life and know the world as it really is, then I must summon up my courage and become a part of it.

Tomorrow, I will go to Annie Calloway.

Christmas Day. The time is early afternoon. I sit here in the storage room recording these brief words before I leave the store. They are also the last words I will write. I have decided it is far too risky for my portfolio of stories to remain here or in the unused cabinet near Stationery, where I have kept them until recently. Who knows who could discover them, and in so doing, learn the secret of the mannequin-turned-man I have become. Therefore, as soon as I am well away from the department store this afternoon, I will discard the portfolio and all its contents in a trash can, never to be found.

As the time draws near for me to go, my expectations soar. Like a child wakening on Christmas morning, I can't help but wonder what surprises and delights await!

But I have carefully prepared myself for my excursion. From the store's information desk, I have taken a city map, and marked the route between the store and

Annie Calloway's apartment. From Gentlemen's Apparel I have borrowed also a splendid chesterfield overcoat, plus a red-and-green silk scarf. From Fine Jewelry, I have removed a pearl necklace, which I will give to Annie as a Christmas gift. From Gourmet Foods, I've taken a plum pudding, given to me by the sales staff, that should complement the dinner she's prepared.

So in a moment I will put on the Chesterfield and the scarf, and with the gifts that I am bringing neatly placed inside a shopping bag, I'll step beyond this store at last. Today, on the most glorious and blessed of holidays, I will give myself the greatest Christmas gift of all—the gift of freedom and the opportunity to truly live!

A Note from the Editor

The account of the individual who identifies himself as Thomas Cavanaugh ends at this point. We publish his so-called story, as well as those of which he claims to be the author, for two reasons: first, that they may entertain the reader and add pleasure to the spirit of the holidays; and second, that one or more of those same readers may have witnessed an incident that happened outside the department store on Christmas Day, and thus be able to furnish the police with information that may aid in their investigation of a crime.

At 12:18 P.M., December 25, a tall man, dressed in a dark chesterfield coat and a red-and-green silk scarf, and carrying a shopping bag of stolen merchandise, attempted to escape the store. He was initially observed by a newly hired guard, loitering inside the hallway near the door used by employees. The new guard became suspicious of the man, and after pretending to be busy at some paperwork, he noticed the man exiting the door.

The guard detained him. He then asked the man's name

and the nature of his business. The man replied that he was Mr. Thomas Cavanaugh, a customer relations representative employed by the store. Thereupon, the guard requested that the man produce his store identification card. He could not.

The guard was in the act of calling store security when the man abruptly bolted through the open doorway and began running down the street. The guard gave chase. Fortunately, a police car had been parked nearby; the two officers witnessed the event, leaped out, and seized the man. They placed him with his arms and legs outspread and facing a display window full of mannequins while they frisked him and took possession of the shopping bag. They were attempting to handcuff him when the man broke free and ran again. The officers pursued him, but by the time they reached the corner where he had turned, no sign of him remained. A canvas of the neighborhood immediately followed, with additional police converging on the scene. In spite of that, he had simply disappeared—or so it seemed.

Still, subsequent investigations have revealed certain facts, which may help to explain the man's behavior. Questioning of store employees confirmed that many of them knew a person who bore a resemblance to the alleged Thomas Cavanaugh, although they were at a loss to say exactly what his job was, or even if he was, in fact, a store employee. Some thought he had been hired on a part-time basis for the holidays, while others believed he was a salesperson of a section different from their own.

As for the name the man gave to the guard, records indicate no person identified as Thomas Cavanaugh has ever been employed by the store. It is assumed to be an alias. Police investigators assume further that the man is a notorious thief, also known as Tommy the Touch, who had gained access to the store, stolen a few items, and was attempting to depart when he was stopped.

Among the contents of the shopping bag he carried was a pearl necklace, a plum pudding, and a leatherbound portfolio. Of these, the last is the most curious. Inside the portfolio, authorities discovered a number of handwritten pages purporting to concern people and events taking place in the department store during the holidays. They show the workings of an overactive mind, and obviously one not wedded to reality. (Can the author actually believe he is a mannequin who has been brought to life each year?)

As for the man's whereabouts, no more is known. Based on information found in the portfolio, however, the police went to the residence of a certain Mrs. Anne Calloway, who until Christmas Eve had been employed as a cleaning woman in the store. They discovered her apartment vacant. The landlord of her building told them that she had had one male visitor on Christmas Day: a tall man in a chesterfield coat. Soon after his arrival, the pair left Mrs. Calloway's apartment, never to return. To this day they remain at large. Although sightings of a happy couple fitting their description continue to be reported, they cannot be confirmed.

So as of this Christmas, the strange case of Thomas Cavanaugh remains unsolved.

And it may for many Christmases to come. . . .

Season's Greetings

from St. Martin's Paperbacks!

A CHRISTMAS GIFT
Glendon Swarthout
On Christmas Eve, on a rural Michigan farm, a young boy and his grandparents discover a special bond, in this enchanting classic of the holiday season.
_____ 92956-0 $4.50 U.S./$5.50 Can.

A CHRISTMAS ROMANCE
Maggie Daniels
Two days before Christmas, a handsome stranger approaches Julia Stonecypher's house with an eviction notice—but Julia is about to discover that Christmas is a time of magic...
_____ 92669-3 $3.99 U.S./$4.99 Can.

A CHRISTMAS LOVE
Kathleen Creighton
Not even the holiday spirit can soften Carolyn Robards' arrogant neighbor—until a Christmastime crisis means they must open their hearts to one another.
_____ 92904-8 $3.99 U.S./$4.99 Can.

Join the world's favorite veterinarian, master storyteller
James Herriot, as he takes us into his wonderful, unique
world, for irrestible, heartwarming tales of animals and
people you will want to read over and over again.

EVERY LIVING THING
_____ 95058-6 $5.99 U.S.

JAMES HERRIOT'S DOG STORIES
_____ 92558-1 $5.99 U.S.